A PUBLISHER'S NOTE

To my dearest readers:

Triple Crown Publications provides you with the best reads in hip-hop fiction. Each novel is hand-selected in its purest form with you, the reader, in mind. *Let That Be the Reason*, an insta-classic, pioneered the hip-hop genre. Always innovative, you can count on Triple Crown's growth: manuscript notes — published books — audio — film.

Triple Crown has also gone international, with novels distributed around the globe. In Tokyo, the books have been translated into Japanese. Triple Crown's revolutionary brand has garnered attention from prominent news media, with features in ABC News, *The New York Times, Newsweek,* MTV, *Publisher's Weekly, The Boston Globe, Vibe, Essence, Entrepreneur magazine, Inc magazine, Black Enterprise magazine, The Washington Post, Millionaire Blueprints magazine* and *Writer's Digest,* just to name a few. I recently earned Ball State University's Ascent Award for Entrepreneurial Business Excellence and was named by Book Magazine as one of publishing's 50 most influential women. Those prestigious honors have taken me from street corner to boardroom accreditation.

Undisputedly, Triple Crown is the leader of the urban fiction renaissance, boasting more than one million sizzling books sold and counting...

Without you, our readers, there is no us,

Vickie Stringer
Publisher

You Knew Betta

BY

CACHET JOHNSON

Compilation and Introduction copyright © 2010 by
Triple Crown Publications
PO Box 247378
Columbus, Ohio 43224
www.TripleCrownPublications.com

Library of Congress Control Number: 2010920094
ISBN 13: 978-09825888-6-4

Author: Cachet Johnson
Graphics Design: Valerie Thompson, Leap Graphics
Photography: Treagen Kier
Editor-in-Chief: Vickie Stringer

First Trade Paperback Edition Printing 2010

10 9 8 7 6 5 4 3 2 1

Printed in the United States of America

Dedication

This book is dedicated to Solomon (Butchie) Hill,
July 23, 1978 – December 23, 2004.

A devoted father, son, brother, uncle, cousin and friend, you
are gone but never forgotten. I love and miss you dearly. Tell
Aunt Darcell and Aunt Deborah that I love them. RIP.

Chapter One

Sasha

"If I have to carry this baby any longer, I'm gonna lose my fuckin' mind!" I yelled at my slow-ass boyfriend, Raimone. "Hurry the hell up!"

I was having my baby today, and I couldn't get to the hospital quick enough. My original due date had been March 19th, and with today being April 2nd, I was two weeks well overdue. So my doctor had scheduled me to be induced.

I had an appointment for 2 p.m.; here it was 1:15, and we're still at the damn house. I was finally going to meet the little girl responsible for packing on all these extra pounds, and I definitely had a couple of words for her for kicking my ass constantly.

I heard Raimone yell from our master bedroom,

"Here I come, Sash. Damn, can't a nigga brush his teeth first?"

My eyes instantly dart to the clock hanging above the entertainment center in the living room; it's now 1:20 p.m. Now he means to tell me, that his ass has been in the bathroom for the past hour, and he's just getting around to brushing his teeth? Taking a rest on the leather loveseat, I lay my head back and exhale because I'm really trying to remain calm.

Men kill me with their attitude. Shit, he acts like he's the one with this huge-ass stomach. I should go in there and pop him upside his head, but that's not going to do anything but slow me up more, so I'll give him a pass today. He betta hurry his monkey ass up, that's for sure!

Look at me running my mouth, and I ain't even introduced myself yet. Well, my name is Sasha Denise Jones. Me and my boyfriend, Raimone LaShawn Ford, have been together for the past seven years. We've been going strong since the summer of 1997 when I was in the tenth grade; and life couldn't be better.

We live in a two-bedroom, two-bath condo in Stone Bridge Towers in downtown Cleveland, Ohio. After trying for about two years to have a baby, we gave up because honestly we didn't think it was our time. We'd just moved into this apartment, and I was still taking morning classes in nursing school, so I guess God saw it fit for us not to have a baby at that time. I've now finished school and have a full-time job as a registered nurse at Metro Health Medical Center. I was there for a little over a year when it happened; finally, we were gonna be parents! I was able to work up until my seventh month, then my doc put me on bedrest outta fear that I may have her early—what a crock of shit!

I was three months pregnant when I had an ultrasound, which said we were having a girl. Raimone couldn't keep the smile off of his face. He said that he always wanted a little girl; he even picked her name out. I was pretty excited. I always wanted a mini-me. I know that babies are not dolls, but I think it would be fun to dress her up in cute little outfits, put bows in her hair. She's going to be just like her momma—a diva!

"Diva" is the correct word for me, because that's exactly what I am. Other than being a big-ass blimp now, I am sexy! I stand at 5'2" and usually I weight around 128 pounds. But right about now I'm weighed-in at a whopping 165! I am the color of caramel, have doe eyes, a button nose, and full lips. I have naturally long eyelashes, so no need for the fake stuff. You can always catch me with my shoulder-length hair in a wrap. I'm hoping that after I drop this load, I'll get my old shape back. I guess we'll just have to wait and see, but until then I'll keep my fingers and my toes crossed.

After another ten minutes had come and gone, Raimone emerged though the door looking like the thug he was. He wore blue Rocawear jeans, a white tee, and a tan Rocawear hoodie. He topped the outfit off with some butter Tims, his signature diamond-studded cross and two-carat studs. My baby always looked his best, and I loved him for that. He was a tall chocolate brotha that I couldn't get enough of. At six-foot-one, Raimone towered over my small frame. He weighed 185 pounds, had dark brown eyes, and had the prettiest lips a woman could ask for. He always wore his hair low cut and lined up. He was pretty much flawless. The only thing that was even close to being a blemish was a scar that he had on his chest from being shot when he was younger.

With all that said—today was not the fucking day! In the real world, I'm about to have this baby and this nigga upstairs is primping like he's heading to the damn club. I mean, I like to look good my damn self, but today I look average because I know there's shit to be done. I have on a pink and white Lady Enyce jogging suit, and all-white Air Force 1's. It's time to go, and I'm ready!

"Damn, baby, why you looking at a nigga like that?" Raimone says with a stupid look on his face. Although I wanted to knock the shit out of him real bad, I kept my cool cause I got his ass!

I struggle to pull myself up off the couch, yelling, "I'm ready to go, and you acting like you're heading to the damn bar! You could've just thrown on anything and brought your ass, I'm ready to end this!" I make the point by gesturing at my massive stomach with one hand while using the other hand to hold on the couch. Rolling my eyes, I grab my pink duffle bag, car keys, and walk out the door. He dutifully follows me after grabbing the rest of my bags for my stay at the hospital. He still had that dumb-ass look on his face, though. I was pissed and he knew it.

He offers lamely, "I'm sorry, Ma, but I couldn't have my daughter coming into this world, and the first thing she sees is her daddy looking busted."

"I'm not laughing, Money, cause the shit is far from funny. Let's just get in the car and go to the hospital." I throw the keys to him to my 2004 smoke-grey Chrysler Sebring convertible; it was a gift from him this past Christmas.

Raimone spent money with no problem, due to him having so much of it. He dabbled into a little bit of everything, from gambling to loaning money at ridiculous rates. Even with all that, most of his money came from drug sales. Back in high school he worked for a guy named Chino and made just enough money to trick-out his car or buy a fly wardrobe. That all quickly changed when Chino took him under his wing.

Chino was a drug lord in the process of moving back to his homeland in Cuba. He wanted someone in the States to keep his business going. He had been watching Raimone for the past few years and saw that he handled his business properly and was never late with his money; basically, he found the perfect student. So for the whole year before Chino was to leave, he prepared Raimone to take over the business; teaching him everything there was to know about the drug game. When he finally left at the end of 1999, Raimone became the new King of Ohio. Chino showed him so much love on the prices of the packages that Raimone was making money hand-over-fist. He went from being a corner boy, to having guys on the corner working for him.

"Why can't we drive my car?" he complains, frowning. He hated to drive my car; he said it made him look like a clown. At this moment I really didn't give a flying fuck about how he felt or looked. If he would've hurried his ass, we could've taken his car. He took his time, not caring about how I felt; so right now, I don't give a shit about his feelings.

"I want to take my car, so let's go," I order, exasperated, standing on the side of my car, waiting for him to open the door. He walks over to the passenger door, opens it, and I climb in, reclining my seat back. Noticing that he's pleading with his eyes, I put on my Chanel glasses so as to let him know that it's the end of the conversation.

Slamming the door, he lifts up the trunk and tosses my bags inside. Then he climbs in the driver seat and starts the engine. "Don't slam my shit no more," I say, nit-picking as we pull off.

To my surprise, we arrive at the hospital right on time, and I am ushered right up to labor and delivery. It takes an hour for me to get in my room, undress, and for the doc to come in and see me. The contractions come as soon as the nurse places oxytocin in my IV, and I'm telling you now that shit ain't no joke! I mean I thought I was gonna fucking die! Before my labor, people used to tell me that the contractions felt like menstrual cramps. Well BULLSHIT, 'cause I ain't never in my life had cramps that bad! I'm laying here right now trying to tough it out for as long as I can, but it's starting to become unbearable. I'm trying to stick to the whole "natural" birth thing, but this is really getting hard. Looking at the small monitor on the side of my bed, I see another contraction coming, so I brace myself. That didn't do any good, because it still hurts like hell. I hold my breath and I squeeze the rails of the bed until my knuckles turn white. I exhale after that one subsides and I start my breathing exercises, thinking that maybe the breathing will help me a little bit. Raimone gets out the chair, walks over to the sink and turns on the water. After wetting a rag he walks over to where I'm laying and dabs the cold cloth across my forehead, making me feel better; I smile at the gesture.

"Ahhh!" I cry out in pain. I can't take this shit no more! The whole "I'm-not-getting-no-drugs" idea flew right out the window. Pushing the "help" button repeatedly, I buzz the nurse so that I can ask for an epidural. Of course they don't give me one right away, saying I had to dilate some more before they could. An hour later, I'm still in pain and no closer to getting the epidural than I was before.

It seems like nurses are going in and out of my room with no care in the world about me. I say loudly, "I promise you I'm gonna go the fuck off, if they come in this mutha'fucka one more time without my epidural!"

"Calm down, Sash, they are only doing their jobs. They can't give it to you right now, so chill out." Raimone was trying to keep the peace—wrong move!

Pushing up on my arms, I sit up slightly and yell in his direction, "Don't you fucking tell me to chill out; you don't know how much pain I'm in. All you doing is sitting your stupid ass over there in the corner watching TV, while I'm over here damn-near dying!" Suddenly another contraction hits me. After that goes away, I start on him again. "So do me a favor and shut the fuck up!" When he doesn't give me the argument I want, I roll over on my side and stare at the monitor once again.

I hear him get out of the chair and walk over to the door. Once I hear the door close, I look up to see that he's gone. I'm pissed and I really want to tell him to go fuck himself, but I'm not about to chase after him. This is the second time that he's showed me that he didn't care about me being angry, the first being when we broke up for a short period of time.

It was two years ago, in October. He disappeared on a Friday night and stayed gone for the whole weekend. I called every jail and hospital in the surrounding counties, searching for him. Saturday afternoon I received a private call. It was him, telling me that he'd gotten pulled over and was taken to jail for a traffic violation. When

I asked him what jail he was in, he told me that he was locked up downtown in the city jail and he wouldn't be released until the morning. Which was a crock of shit, because I had called down there numerous times, so I knew he wasn't there. I told him that whatever bitch he was with to enjoy himself, and when he decided to come home I wouldn't be there. I guess he thought I was bullshitting because he didn't attempt to come home at all that night.

When he came home the next day, he found the house empty. I packed up all of my stuff and moved back home with my parents. It took him a couple of days to track me down due to me not answering any of his calls. But after awhile he convinced me to come back home, telling me that he was sorry and promising that he'd never do anything again to jeopardize our future.

As more contractions started to come, I remain quiet. My tears flow on to the while hospital pillow. I see the doc enter the room with a smile on his face. He's an older white gentleman, tall with a slim build. His jet-black hair is cut short and looks like it's been dyed to hide the grey.

"Hello, Miss Jones. I'm Dr. Tate, and I'm here to check on how much you've dilated," he said while sliding his hands into a pair of gloves.

I take a breath and grab the rails so that I can turn over onto my back. Placing both of my legs into the stirrups, I allow him to check me out. It's funny how you don't give a damn who sees you naked when you're about to have a baby. You're free to spread your legs at the drop of a dime. I'm ready for the pain to be over; I want to hold my baby.

"Owwww," I groan, biting down on my lip. It feels

as if he's sticking his whole arm up in my shit!

"Miss Jones, you're only three centimeters. You have to get to at least seven before you can get the epidural," he tells me, smiling once again. He removes the gloves, tossing them into the wastebasket, washes his hands and walks out of the door. Maybe five minutes later, in walks Raimone, but I lay back in the bed pretending to be preoccupied with the TV.

"I'm sorry," I hear him say as he hands me a cup of ice chips; that must have been why he had left. I place a couple of them into my dry mouth, making a crunching sound as I bite down on them.

"Sorry for what?" I was actually happy that he'd come back, but I wasn't going to let him know it.

"For being inconsiderate. I know you're in a lot of pain and if you wanna flip out, you go right ahead." He sits on the edge of the bed; I scoot over to give him more room. "Roll over on your side." I start to ask him why, but instead I grab on to the rail and do as he suggests. He unties the strings on the back of my gown, causing them to fall open and expose my naked back. I close my eyes and enjoy the massage that he gives me; I love my baby.

Almost two hours later, Dr. Tate finally gives staff the "go" for my epidural. An anesthesiologist walks in with this gigantic needle while the nurse tells Raimone that he has to step out for a moment while they give me my shot. Once he's outside the door, I get into a sitting position with one nurse holding each of my hands. I'm scared, but I don't move because if I do, the needle could hit a nerve and temporarily paralyze me; they didn't have to tell me that warning twice! Taking a deep breath, I feel a small pinch in the lower part of my back when the needle goes in; it didn't hurt bad at all. With the help of the nurses I lay back down on my pillow and they allow Raimone to come back inside.

Raimone stayed by my side the entire time, coaching me on. Even though he helped me out a lot, I ain't gonna even lie, there were times when I wanted to tell him to shut the fuck up with all that "keep breathing" shit; but I didn't. I chuckle at the thought of Raimone passing out, which could have been on his mind, from the way he was looking. He was making so many faces, and sweating so hard you would've thought he was having the baby.

Several hours later, I give the final push and out came my beautiful bundle of joy. She was gorgeous! Raisha LaShawna Ford entered the world on April 2, 2004 at 11:05 p.m. She weighed 7 pounds, 3 ounces, was 19 ½ inches long and had a head full of curly black hair. Raisha didn't look identical to either of her parents; she actually looked like a mix of both. She was going to be her father's complexion, and I knew that because I checked behind her ears, and they were a little on the dark side. She had my eyes and nose; but other than that, she was all her dad. She even had his small ears.

Raimone's face as he held our daughter will forever be etched in my mind. He looked amazed, and I believe I even saw a tear drop.

"Thank you," he says to me, handing the baby over to the nurse.

"For what?" I ask.

"For giving me a beautiful daughter and making me the happiest man on Earth," he answers quietly. "Seeing you give birth strengthened the love that I have for you. I already loved you so deeply, but now I love you even more." He was looking directly into my eyes. I'm exhausted, but I quickly shake it off when I see him reach into his pocket while getting down on one knee.

Covering my mouth with both of my hands I say, "Oh, my God!" In his hand he holds a small velvet box. When he opens it, I see that inside there's a 3-carat, princess-cut solitary diamond ring.

"Sasha Denise Jones, will you make my life complete by accepting my proposal to be my wife?" he proposes with tears in his eyes. I couldn't contain my excitement as I said "yes" numerous times, just to make sure he heard me.

"Congratulations!" the hospital staff cries out as they applaud.

"Thank you," we both say in unison. You couldn't wipe the smile off of my face if you tried as I showed all thirty-two of my pearly whites. I'm finally going to marry the man I love; I can't wait until the day.

Fatigue started to take over; I was getting sleepier by the minute. Giving up the fight to stay awake, I drift into a satisfying sleep. As I doze off, I am thinking about how wonderful life is going to be. But who among us at such moments ever takes into consideration that life doesn't always go as planned.

Chapter Two

Sasha

It's been two years and life couldn't get any better for us. I'm now 24 and a wife and mother. We got married last year and moved out of our small apartment. That place was cool when it was just us two, but with Raisha growing up so fast, we had to upgrade. The house-hunt didn't take too long and soon we relocated to Strongsville, Ohio, which is a lot closer to my twin sister Tasha. It's not that much further away from where we used to live, but it's gratefully out of the inner city. We now live in a four- bedroom, three-and-a-half bath brick house that I absolutely love. There's more than enough room in the backyard for Raisha to run around. She turned two last week, and we had a blast at the birthday party.

We threw the party in the backyard of our house,

because there is plenty of room back there. Raimone rented a lot of tables and chairs for about 100 guests. I'm glad he did, because everyone we invited showed up. The kids had fun running in and out of the playhouses and pop-up tunnels, but they lost their minds when SpongeBob and Patrick came out. Raimone rented the characters because he knows that Raisha loves them; I swear she has every DVD ever made, and her TV is always on NICK. I have never seen my daughter smile so much. She was so happy to see all of our friends and family, and it warmed my heart to see her happy face.

She did pretty well on birthday gifts. She got a Dora the Explorer bike, a Barbie Beetle power wheel, kitchen and table set, a toy WhirlPool washer and dryer, a vanity, a few Cabbage Patch Kids, a radio, a few DVDs, some Barbies with the doll house and over 100 outfits, and her daddy bought her a 32" Plasma. No, I don't know what the hell a two-year-old would need with a Plasma TV, so you need to ask her dad that. She had two sheet cakes, one Dora and the other was SpongeBob. Like I said we had a ball, even the grown folks.

Right now I'm sitting in the house staring aimlessly at the TV, watching an Old Navy commercial. I'm waiting on Tasha's slow ass, because we are supposed to be going to the Mirage tonight; which is a club in the flats that we go to from time to time   I haven't been in a nice while, because I've been doing the family thing; I'm just not digging the club scene anymore. That's exactly what I told Tasha; but after listening to her whine about how I haven't been spending time with her, I agreed. She told me that she would be here early, but knowing Tasha she'll be late as always. I don't know why I always fall for it, the next time we supposed to go somewhere, I'm gonna take my time getting ready. Of course you know that's when she'll be here on time.

Just like I expected she would, she rings the door bell almost two hours later. After opening the door I give her a once over. She just recently cut all of her hair off in a short bob, and it was dyed jet black. It was silky straight and had a shine to it, letting you know it was healthy, and her make-up was flawless. Ms. Hot Ass had on skin-tight Baby Phat blue jeans with a gold cat on the pocket, the matching jacket, and a white and gold Baby Phat belly shirt that showed off her diamond star belly ring. On her feet were a pair of gold pumps that matched the gold satchel on her arm.

"Don't ask me to go out no more," I say, not giving her a chance to say anything.

"Why?" she asks, placing her hands on her hips, causing the gold bangles on her arms to clang.

"You know damn well what I'm talking about. You beg me to go out with you, then you got me sitting around waiting on yo' slow ass," I complain. "I don't know why you even give somebody a time when you know you ain't gone be here. I should just stay home and let yo' ass go out by yo' damn self!"

"Well damn, tell me how you really feel," she pouts.

Laughing out loud, I roll my eyes and step back to allow her to come into the house. "Bitch, you get on my nerves."

"Don't hate on all this, with yo' jealous ass. You just mad because I look better then you, ugly bitch!" She moves her hands across her body in a seductive way.

Even though we're identical twins, this bitch really thinks she looks better than me, ain't that some shit?

Our height and weight are exactly the same, especially now that I'm back to 128 pounds. Boy am I happy to be back at my pre-baby weight, because I don't think I could've made it being a chubby chick.

Turning her nose up like something stinks she looks hard at me and says, "I know that's not what you wearing." Ha! This bitch is really tripping now because I know I look good. I'm rocking the shit out of this Akademiks outfit, which consists of a pair of tight dark blue jeans, and a red loose-neck half sweater with a logo on front that hung off one shoulder.

Because I didn't get any stretch marks after having Raisha, I put my tight abs on display. I got on my brand new knee-high red leather Nine West boots that I picked up from the mall a couple weeks ago. I'm hoping like hell that they don't make my feet hurt late, cause that would not be a good look. I hate seeing a hoe walking in the club with no shoes on; how tacky is that? They cool right now, but you know how it is when you wear a new pair of shoes; I should've broken these bitches in first. Anyway, with my diamond heart necklace, diamond encrusted hoops, wedding ring, and two diamond tennis bracelets, I was shitting on these hoes! My brown hair had just gotten streaked blonde and I let it hang loosely past my shoulder blades. I knew I was stepping the fuck out, so I didn't care what she had to say.

"Where's my Rai-Rai!" Tasha yells through the house. She loves Raisha with all her heart and will do anything for her, because she says she'll never have children of her own. Something about not wanting to share everything she has with another person; the bitch is just selfish, if you ask me.

The next thing I know, Raisha is flying down the

hallway in her Dora pajamas, screaming, "Auntie, Auntie!" When she finally gets close enough, she jumps mid-air and lands in Tasha's arms. Tasha smothers her with kisses for at least a minute straight before she puts her down.

Opening her purse, she searches around in it before saying, "Look what Auntie got for her baby." She hands Raisha a small box with a pair of small gold Dora the Explorer earrings. Excitedly Raisha quickly gives Tasha a kiss and then runs down the hall to show her daddy the new gift.

Shaking my head I warn, "If you buy her one more damn thing."

"Bitch please! That's my only niece and if I wanna spoil her, I'm gonna spoil her. Besides I know yo' ass ain't talking with all the shit y'all buy her."

"Shut up!" was all I could say, 'cause I knew she was right.

Coming out of the room dressed in a white wife beater and some basketball shorts, Raimone says, "What's up, Tasha?"

"Shit, just doing me and dodging these lames." She replies as she sits on the couch rummaging through her purse looking for something.

"That's cool, but don't make this here a habit." He says winking at me. I laugh inside because I know that he's trying to make her mad.

"Make what a habit?" Tasha asks, pulling out a pair of signature Baby Phat earrings. Glancing my way with a look of confusing on her face, she puts an earring in each of her ears. I avoid her gaze by looking down at my fresh French manicure.

"This club-hopping shit," Raimone explains. "Sasha

is a married woman now. She supposed to be at home, not at the club acting whorish."

Tasha jumps up from the couch so fast she drops the matching necklace on the floor. "Raimone gone with all that bullshit! Nigga what about you, don't yo' ass go to clubs and ain't you married?"

"Don't question me, woman!" Not able to act mad any longer, he laughed.

Tasha bends down to pick up her necklace and puts it on while walking toward to the door. "Boy bye with yo' silly ass!"

"See ya! Y'all be careful out there, baby," Ramoine tells me as I wrap my arms around his neck and give him a succulent kiss on the lips. After smacking me on my ass, he turns and heads back into the bedroom. "Have fun!" I hear him say as I grab my red clutch and walk out the door.

By the time we got to the club, it was well after twelve, because we had to pick up our cousin Keisha from our Aunt Monica's house. Keisha Marie Jones, who we all called "Keish," is our father's sister's only child. She wasn't only our cousin—she was also our best friend. Born only ten days apart, we were more like triplets. When we were younger, people would call us "Three the Hard Way" Because we caused so much ruckus everywhere we went. But, hey, that was just us, I guess.

Keisha was a beautiful girl, caramel colored, light brown eyes, standing around 5'4"; at 145 pounds, she was thicker than Tasha or me. She always wore her honey blonde hair in a Halle Berry cut, and trust me she wore it well. Tonight she had on a pink cat suit, with some black thigh-high boots, and a black half jacket. As she walked towards the club, all you heard were niggas yelling about her big-ass booty. That girl had more ass then the law allowed. She had so much she could give me and Tasha most of it and still have plenty.

The club was packed! Believe me, there was muthafuckas wall to wall. There were bitches dancing on top of the speakers that were in each corner of the dance floor. This one chick had the nerve to be up there in a short-ass skirt with no fucking panties! What the hell was wrong with these desperate bitches these days? The killer was the fact that she was showing off those raggedy-ass thighs like her shit was cute; all I could do was shake my head. After getting a drink at the bar, we took a seat over at a booth in the corner to soak up the scene. I was looking in awe at how some of these people came outside; people would wear anything! Bitches were walking past me with their hair jelled back, and I swear I saw a girl with her hair in a fan—what the fuck?

"I'm a nice dude, with some nice dreams. See these ice cubes, see these Ice Creams? Eligible bachelor, million-dollar boat, that's whiter then what's spilling down your throat."

"That's my shit!" Keish yells as we all get up and head toward the dance floor.

As soon as our feet hit the floorboards, guys are grabbing at us trying to get a dance. Snatching my arm away from some dreadlock-wearing nigga, I look over to see Keish and Tasha grinding and shaking their asses up on some dudes; they were being a little too touchy-feely for me.

"When the pimp's in the crib, Ma; Drop it like it's hot, drop it like it's hot, drop it like it's hot. When the pigs try to get at you; Park it like it's hot, Park it like it's hot, Park it like it's hot…."

I'm on the floor fucking up that dance ole' girl was doing in the video when I feel someone come up behind me and start to dance. Turning around ready to flip out, I see that the guy isn't bad looking and I finish doing my thing. We dance for three songs straight before I walk away; it's hot in this damn sweater!

Desperately needing to cool off, I walk off the dance floor in search of a seat on the patio. I'm getting irritated because it's taking me forever to get outside—I was bumping into so many people. Everybody in this bitch is either smoking a cigarette or black and mind, so my eyes are starting to burn.

Apparently, I bump into this one girl too hard; I heard her say something smart. Not thinking anything of it I kept it moving, not even bothering to look back. I had better shit to do with my time than to be arguing at the club. I quicken my pace when I see an available seat right in the front of the patio, until I feel someone tap me on my shoulder. Thinking it was some bug-a-boo-ass nigga, I spin around ready to tell him to step the fuck off; I'm greeted by a light-skinned chick with red hair.

"Excuse you!" she yells over the music.

"What?" I asked, confused. Who the fuck was this chick, and what did she want?

"I said 'excuse you'; you bumped into me back there." She rolled her neck, and pointed to where I guess she was when I bumped her.

I know the look on my face has got to be priceless; she can't be real. "Are you serious?" I asked, standing akimbo, not believing that this bitch was really tripping on a little bump. It wasn't that fucking serious, if you ask me. Hell, you bump into a million people at the club, and nobody comes up to you talking shit.

"Yes the fuck I am, bitch. Now say 'excuse me'!" she yelled once again, this time putting her finger in my face. Now I'm not sure what she was looking for, but she's defiantly about to get it. Her putting her finger in my face is about to get her in a world of trouble. I take a deep breath, because I'm really trying to remain calm. I don't think she knows just how close she is to getting the shit beat out of her. That's why I knew that this girl didn't know me from Adam, because people who know me know that I don't play with these hands. I mean who the fuck comes up to confront you about bumping them in a crowded-ass club? By then, Keish and Tasha have come over to the scene this bitch was causing, trying to see what the hell was going on.

"What's up, Sash, you gotta problem?" Tasha asks, looking back and forth from me to light skin.

"Naw, I'm not the one with the problem, ole' girl is," I calmly say, pointing to the mystery woman.

The next thing I know, I'm seeing stars. That bitch swung, hitting me square in the eye; I was stunned.

Quickly regaining my composure, I hit her with a mean right that connected with her chin, causing her to stumble a bit. I follow up with a series of punches that land her flat on her ass, dazed and confused. Taking my gaze off of her for a minute I notice Keish working the fat hoe that was with her, while Tasha was damn near stomping someone I assume was her other friend. Those couple of seconds gave light skin the time she needed to get back up on her feet and steal me in the face. Jumping back, she posted up and threw a quick left but missed. I didn't when I followed up with a jab that busted her lip.

I was trying to rearrange her fucking face; I don't play that shit! She had punched the shit out of me, and I wanted her ass to pay for my pain, cause that shit really hurt.

She was trying her best to hang, and I can honestly say she was giving me a run for my money. What she didn't know was that I also like to wrestle; she quickly found this out once I got a good grip and body slammed her. Hearing the security guards rushing through the gathering crowd, I quickly climb on top of her and get in as many licks as I can before they break up the fight. Of course I didn't get too many in, because before I knew it, I was being lifted up in mid-air and carried to the front door kicking and screaming.

My hair was all over my damn head and the neck of my sweater was stretched out due to her pulling on it. I'm so fucking embarrassed, because this is not me at all. Fighting in the club is for these hood-rat-ass hoes, and trust me when I tell you that I'm far from one of those. I mean I get down if need be, but I don't go around fighting like I did when I was a teenager. Back then all you had to do was look at me wrong and I was getting in yo' ass like hemorrhoids! I'm grown now with a daughter and a husband at home; I got too much class! Like Adele Givens says, "I'm such a fuckin' lady!"

We were tripping the whole ride home about the drama at the club, trying to figure out what was up. Neither one of us could see what this bitch was so mad for. It was puzzling.

"She cold-cocked the shit outta yo' ass, man!" Tasha cracks, moving her arms like ole' girl. "She was like, bam!"

"Yeah she did, but she got what she came for when I

tore dat ass up!" I say, getting pumped all over again.

"Fuck what y'all talking bout, that fat outta-shape bitch made me lose my damn earring," Keisha pouted. "Do you know how much those bitches cost?" Not waiting for our reply, she continued, "Seven hundred mutha'fuckin dollars, I should tell you to turn around so I can beat her ass again. I really liked those earrings."

"Don't worry bout it, cuz; I'll buy you another pair. Fuck them hoes," I tell her. Looking into the rearview mirror, I see her in the back seat cheesing like a Cheshire cat. When she saw me looking, she put back on a serious face. I laugh at the fact that I fell right into her trap. "I can't stand yo' ass!"

"What?" she asks innocently, and we all bust out laughing. She knew that if she pouted long enough, I'd buy her another pair; these hoes knew me too well.

I dropped them both off and I was finally home to face Raimone. He hated it when I fought, and when he was around, he did his best to stop me from getting angry. He knew that I was loose cannon, due to the fact that I've snapped on him a time or two. Either way, I didn't feel like hearing his damn mouth. All of the lights were off outside, so I figured he was sleeping. Boy, was I wrong. He was wide awake, and by the look on his face he noticed my eye. All I could do was hold my breath and wait for the storm.

Chapter Three

Naitaisha

I knew I would run into that bitch one day. I just didn't know it would be tonight at the club. I tried to knock that hoe's head clean off her body! Waltzing around the club like her shit don't stink. What the fuck ever! My lip's busted, I got a migraine out of this world, and a couple of scratches on my face—but it was well worth it. She fucked my do up—ole' hair-pulling-ass bitch! The only real thing that I'm salty about is the fact that I couldn't do her dirty like I really wanted to. That ole' none-fighting-ass hoe, gone slam me. What type of shit is that? Who the hell did she think she was, a fucking pro wrestler? Seeing that she couldn't go head-up with me, she had to try something different.

Those big dumb security guards put a damper on my

plans. She was lucky I couldn't get to my knife quick enough, or she would've been sliced the fuck up! Yeah, they say you can't bring weapons inside the club, but they ain't as smart as they think they are, cause I damn sho did! All the perverted security guards do is check women's purses and run a hand-held metal detector across the front of our bodies, stopping a little too long on our titties. I'm so much smarter then they are, though, because I put my small knife in the crack of my ass— with it being so big, no one notices a thing.

It's funny, 'cause she has no clue who I am. I honestly don't give a fuck if she does; I'm tired of sharing. I've been playing second-fiddle to her for the past three and a half years, and I've grown sick of it. He at home with that bitch and their daughter every night. While I'm with our daughter, tucking her in by my damn self. I bet that bitch really think she got something special, which I know for damn sure it ain't. What she don't know is that while her daughter just turned two, mine's was almost three.

Yep, that's right, I got his first child. My daughter's name is Raimona LaShawnte Ford, just like her daddy. Ha-ha, bitch! You can look crazy all you want, but I don't give a damn! You don't know what the fuck I been though, so who are you to judge? You're probably sitting on yo' damn couch reading this, eating chips and shit without a care in the world.

Because you're gonna be all up in my business, I might as well be the person to share it with you. Just to make sure you get the right version of the story, and not the bullshit!

I am Naitaisha Latriese Bolen, and I am 22 years old. I'm 5'5", 120 pounds, and I consider myself a dime. I'm the color of butter, have small upslanted eyes, a slender nose, and thin lips. I have really small breasts, only wearing a 32B. But where I lack in one department, I make up for in another. Let me just put it like this, my measurements are 32-20-40. That's right, I have more than enough ass to go around and if you don't think that's good enough, I got some bomb-ass pussy! My best feature is my fire-red hair that hangs down the middle of my back; yes, I'm a bad bitch!

So why am I sharing a man, you say? I couldn't even begin to tell you. I guess I'm a fool for love, if that's even a real thing. Let me start from the beginning, so maybe you can see my position more clearly.

I met Raimone a little less than four years ago on a hot August day, at a basketball game in the hood. When I first saw him I really wasn't impressed. I mean he was a cutie and all, but I wasn't the type to fall all over no nigga. Well, anyways, when the game was over, he strolled over and asked me if he could talk to me for a minute. After I told him that he could, we chit-chatted for a while as he walks me to my car. He told me his name and a little bit about himself. I told him a couple of things also, and we decided to exchange phone numbers.

We talked on the phone a few times, getting to know each other a little bit more. I learned that he was a hustler, which I kinda figured anyways; I can spot one a mile away. Then he went on to tell me that he didn't need to get his hands dirty; he had other people to do that for him. He asked me out and I agreed to let him take me out for a bite to eat. Our first date consisted of us going to the Olive Garden. It was pretty nice, and he was a complete gentleman the whole time. After about two months I decided to go ahead and give him the goodies. Big mistake! After that night we would be forever connected.

It was a Friday night when he called me and told me to pack up a swimsuit and some overnight clothes. He picked me up and took me to the Marriott on West 150th. We got our room key and headed up to the room, which was beautiful. Once in the room we changed into our swim gear and headed downstairs to the pool. It was so much fun; we played in the water and everything. He totally ruined my fresh wrap by dunking me under the water. When he noticed that I was upset, he assured me not to worry because he would pay to get it done again. By the time we returned to the room, I was so fucking horny it was ridiculous. The room we had was equipped with a Jacuzzi, so I ran some water and placed the bottle of wine that he brought into the tub of ice. Not the least bit ashamed of my body, I stripped down to my bare ass and climbed in. Apparently Raimone felt the same way because he soon followed my lead; and boy, was I pleased.

When he was standing before me completely naked, I noticed that he had a nice muscular build and was cut in all the right places. I mean you could tell that he had a nice body with his clothes on, but not as nice as it looked with they were removed. My mouth watered as I looked down and saw that he was packing about 9 ½ inches of chocolate that I couldn't wait to taste. After he climbed in, I went to touch the scar that he had on his chest, and he grabbed my arm and pulled me in for a deep kiss. I didn't stop him, because I wanted it just as bad as he did, if not more. I pushed him back into a sitting position and mounted him, never once breaking the kiss.

We fucked hard until the water turned cold, and neither one of us thought about using protection. I don't think we got a wink of sleep the whole night; we were too busy doing the nasty. The next morning came and went, and we ended up staying at the hotel for another night. Most of the morning was spent sleeping, because we were both so tired from the night before. Raimone only left my side for a split second, and that was when he went into the hallway to make a phone call, which he told me was important business. I didn't trip, because the damn thing had been ringing all day and night. I had my thoughts that maybe it was his girlfriend or something, but I didn't ask and he didn't tell.

I honestly didn't give two shits if he did a girlfriend; it was none of my concern. If he did, that was her problem, because at that point in time, he was with me. It was a day filled with banging-ass sex, and I wasn't complaining. After about ten minutes on the phone he returned, and we finished were we left off. We ordered room service, and after we were done eating, we were back at it. We sucked and fucked each other for the remainder of the day; I was hooked.

The next morning he dropped me off at my apartment, and told me to call him later. As promised, he gave me some money to get my hair done; well, to be exact, he handed me $400. I walked all the way to my front door with a smile on my face; I had found my new Boo.

After that weekend he came over all of the time, and it was like a fairy tale. He'd come over every weekday morning and stay until the mid-afternoon. He told me he did this because on the weekends he was tied up handling business. We'd sometimes catch an early movie or go out to breakfast. He made sure I had everything that I needed without me having to ask; which was a big bonus in my eyes. He was so nice and sweet, nothing like the other guys that I fucked around with. Back then I was used to niggas only coming around when they wanted to fuck, never spending time or taking me anywhere. It didn't bother me, though; as long as they made sure my pockets were laced, it was fine. Raimone was different.

I kinda thought that maybe he had a girlfriend, because after the first time we hooked up, he could never spend the night. He didn't really come over late in the evening and if he did, he didn't stay long. I talked to him a little bit on Saturdays; but on Sundays I didn't get so much as a phone call, because he told me that Sunday that was his busiest day. Once again, I didn't trip. I figured he was spending so much time with me, what time could he give someone else? If he did have someone at home, she was stupid as hell, because there was no way my man would be gone every morning with no damn job. We were doing so well for a good two months! That was, until I noticed that I had missed my period. After heading to my doctor's office and confirming what I already knew, I was in a tight spot. Once I got back home, I immediately called Raimone, and told him the news.

"Hello," Raimone answered on the second ring.

"Hey, Mone, it's me, Naitaisha," I said nervously.

"Boo, I know who you are. What's up?"

"I'm pregnant!" I blurted out, without thinking. Shit, I didn't have time to beat around the bush. It had to be done.

"What!" he yelled.

"I said I'm pregnant, seven weeks to be exact." All I

heard was silence. "Hello," I asked again.

"Yeah, I'm here man, how much do you need?" I was crushed. I mean, I know he wasn't my man, but he'd been acting like it for the past few months; what the fuck!

"What do you mean, how much do I need? Who said I was getting an abortion?" I asked, getting heated. Who the fuck did he think he was? This was my got damn body.

"But — " he blurted out.

"But what?" I asked.

"I got a girl; and if she finds out, she gonna kill me," he admitted.

I remember my throat being dry after hearing that, so I went into the kitchen to get a bottled water. "You picked a fine time to tell me that shit! How long have y'all been together?"

"Come on now, Taisha, with that bullshit," Raimone said, " 'cause you know you ain't never asked me. If you assumed, then that's yo' fault; but miss me with all that loud talking. We been together for six years and I can't risk her leaving me; I love her."

Ain't that a bitch? It's crazy how men will wine and dine you, spend time with you, fuck yo' pussy until it's dry and then want to tell you that they love their girl. It's like, where the fuck was all that love for her when you was all up in my guts, you nasty bastard!

I wanted to cry, but he was right. I never asked him if he had a woman, because at the time I didn't care. Even then, it was one thing to think he had a woman, but it's a whole different story now that I knew he had one. Then for him to sit on the phone and tell me that he can't risk her leaving him only made me feel worse.

I usually don't mind when dudes tell me that they have somebody at home, because with me it's all about the cast; I like Raimone.

I took a deep breath and said to him, "I'm having my baby and it really don't matter if you want me to or not." I wasn't changing my mind.

"I'm saying, you don't need no baby right now," Raimone argued.

I flipped out. "You don't know what the fuck I need, so please spare me with the bullshit! You're not looking out for me, you're looking out for your damn self. So don't sit on this phone acting like you're oh-so-worried about my well being!" I cried into the phone; my feelings were hurt.

"Man, I ain't ready for no kids," he wailed.

"You ain't ready for no kids? Did you think about that when you was sliding yo' dick up in me raw? Did you say that when you didn't even attempt to pull out? Instead, you busted all up in me. No, you didn't. So don't say the shit now." He was really getting on my fucking nerves, playing the victim.

"You right, you're absolutely right. I'm not gonna lie and say that I don't care about you, because I do. I actually care about you a lot." That brought a smile to my face.

"I care about you too, but I'm having my baby," I said emphatically.

"The deal is this," Raimone countered. "You have the baby, and I will provide everything both of you need. After the baby is born, I'll move you into a house and out of that small apartment. You just have to promise me that you won't let this get back to my girl. Do we have a deal?"

"So basically, you want us to be your secret family, that you take care of?" I asked, making sure that I completely understood what he was saying.

"Don't think of it as being my secret family. Think of it as kind of like my extended family." He was playing word games like I was stupid. I knew what the hell he meant, but I agreed to it anyway. What he didn't know was, that in the back of my mind, I was sure that I was going to win him over, and take him from the bitch that he claimed to love.

I called myself being the perfect "side line." I fucked him when he wanted to be fucked, and I sucked his dick at the drop of the dime. Doing everything he asked me to, just to prove myself. I never questioned him about what he was doing, and I very rarely called to ask for any of his time. I acted like I really didn't give a fuck, when in fact I was dying inside. I went through all of the important stages of my pregnancy alone, even giving birth with just my mother in the delivery room. I cried many nights thinking about him lying in the bed with her, while I was alone. Just the thought of him touching her made me sick to my stomach; but what could I do? After awhile I just got used to it and completely started to ignore him. I wouldn't call him at all and when he called me, I made myself unavailable; I was tired of playing by his rules.

Seeing that I wasn't studding his ass, he made a change for the better. He started coming around a lot more and telling me how much he cared for me; once again, I was sucked back in. I thought that eventually we would be a happy family, but that day has yet to come. That was two years ago and nothing has changed. I've been in this fucked-up situation ever since! The part that screwed me up the most is the fact that he up and married this bitch; that broke my fucking heart!

Here I am being the ride-or-die bitch that you want me to be, but you up and put a ring on this hoe's finger? Was there something wrong with me that I didn't know about? If so, please tell me.

I'm a soldier, though, 'cause Raimone loves me. I know he does. It's just that bitch who is in the way. Without her, it'll be him, me, and Raimona—a happy family, and I know this. Now don't get me wrong, he provides for the both of us, so I can't complain. He did just as he said he would and moved us out of my low-income apartment and into a three-bedroom house off of W. 130th in Bellaire, on Tyler street. He bought me a new Chevy Tahoe, and he keeps me and Moni laced in the flyest shit. He always comes over and gives us a lot of his time, but not the amount of time I want. I love him with all my heart and I know that one day he will come around. I just have to wait it out, even though I'm not sure how much longer it will be. Realizing that I haven't talked to him all day, I stretch my arm toward my nightstand to grab the phone. I'm going to call him and see if he'll come over tonight, because I really need some dick right about now.

"Hey baby, it's me. Call me when you get a chance. Moni and I miss you; we haven't seen you all week. I love you, bye." But I was only speaking to his voicemail, because he didn't answer. Yeah, he'll come around. I just have to sit and wait. Until then, I'm going to make that bitch's life as miserable as I possibly can.

Chapter Four

Sasha

"What the hell happened to your face, Sash?" Raimone asks with a crazed expression.

"I got into a fight at the club," I say nonchalantly, as I attempt to walk past him.

"What the fuck you mean, you got into a fight at the club? You got a damn black eye, who the fuck was you fighting, a dude?" he asks, blocking my path so that he can examine my face.

I went on to explain to him exactly what happened, and he was just as confused as I was. We end up chalking her up as a hating-ass bitch.

After a while, Raimone calms down, and starts laughing at my eye. He said it looked like I put a round in with Holyfield. I laughed also and assured him, as I showed him a couple of my moves, that I beat the brakes off that hoe. After clowning with his ass for about an hour, I kiss Raisha and go to take a shower. The hot water feels good on my body as it releases all of the stress that the day has brought. Putting my hair directly under the stream, I allow it to become soaked as I pour a nice amount of shampoo into the palm of my hand. I close my eyes while working up a lather, trying to rid my hair of the smoke from the club. Once I'm satisfied, I step back under the spray and rinse the shampoo out. Taking my bath sponge off of the hook, I foam it up and clean my body from top to bottom and watch as the water washes all of the dirt away.

Turning off the water, I take hold of my head towel and wrap it tightly around my dripping hair. I then pull my body towel off the hook on the back of the bathroom door and proceed to dry droplets of water from my skin. Standing in front of the mirror, I towel-dry the rest of the loose water from my hair before I brush it into a tight bun and place a cotton scarf around it. I sit on the edge of the bed and rub my body down with Johnson's Baby Lotion, before sliding into the bed naked. Wrapping my arms snuggly around Raimone, I kiss him softly on his back. My head barely hit the pillow before I was out like a light; tonight was exhausting.

A small ray of sum snuck through the window causing me to wake up a little bit earlier then I wanted. Looking at the digital clock on the nightstand, I see that it's only 7:30 in the morning. Rubbing my eyes, I sit up and slowly climb out of the bed, careful not to wake Raimone. Opening up my pajama drawer, I grab my Mickey Mouse nightgown and head into the bathroom. Sitting on the toilet I exhale as I relieve myself of the pee that I'd been holding for the past few hours. Taking some tissue I wipe myself and stand up, flushing the toilet behind me. After brushing my teeth and washing my face, I saunter into the kitchen to make both my babies breakfast.

An hour later, as I'm reaching into the cabinet for the plates, Raimone walks into the kitchen with my princess in his arms.

"You need some help, sexy?" he asks.

"No, I got it, baby," I assure him.

After placing her in the high chair, he pours all three of us a glass of orange juice, while I rinse the plates and dry them with the dishtowel. I pile bacon, sausage, scrambled eggs, grits, home fries, and a couple of hotcakes on mine and Raimone's plates; then I start on Raisha's. Using her SpongeBob dish set, I give her two small pancakes, some home fries, and a sausage link. Scooping up a healthy spoonful of grits, I pour it into the bowl and place it in front of her, sprinkling a small amount of sugar on top of it. Before I sit down, I grab the syrup out of the cabinet, and the ketchup from the fridge; as I scoot my chair closer to the table, we bow our heads.

"Precious Lord, we truly thank you for the food we are about to receive, for the nourishment of our bodies. Christ sake, Amen," I say, leading grace.

We eat in a statisfied silence, until Raisha starts laughing. I look up just in time to see Raimone with his hand shaped in an "O" around his eye. That bastard was making fun of me again, and I wasn't having it.

"Go ahead and laugh at your daddy, baby. We'll see who gets the last one," I say to her as I give him a sly wink.

Raimone stopped chewing and asks, "What you mean by that?"

"Don't worry about it, you will see. I got yo' ass!" I promise him as I get up to empty our plates and place the few dishes in the dishwasher. He wasn't laughing anymore; he knew exactly what I was referring to. It's so funny how nigga's bitch up when you take the pussy from their ass: oh yeah, I got him right where I want him.

He gets up from the table and stands directly behind me at the sink, pressing his dick against my ass. "Baby, don't be like that, you know I love's my baby." He slowly wraps his arms around my waist, pulling me closer.

I close my eyes as he gently nibbles on the back of my neck. See he was playing unfair now, because he knows that's my sweet spot. He continues to touch and rub my body as I continue to load the dishes, pretending like it's not affecting me.

"Get yo' hands off me, and get your daughter out of the highchair, you damn freak!" I smile, laughing as I swat his hands away. He walks away to get Raisha, but not before smacking me hard on the ass. He knew damn well that it hurt, because I didn't have any panties on under my nightgown. He wants me to chase him, but I had better things to do.

I finish up in the kitchen and join them in the living room, and just as I suspected, Raisha was knocked out on a blanket laid on the loveseat, while her dad was on the sofa watching Sports Center on our plasma.

"Come here, baby," Raimone beckons me as he pats the couch beside him. I oblige and put my feet up on his lap. He gently massages both my feet, while I pretend to watch the TV. Slowly he works his way up my leg, and all the way up my thigh; I close my eyes because it feels so good. Before I know it, he is up under my nightgown, fondling between my legs, and I'm loving every minute of it. I throw my head back and open my legs wider, as he rubs my clit in a circular motion, causing me to bite down on my bottom lip. My legs start to shake because I'm about to cum, but he abruptly stops.

My eyes pop open and I look at him like he's gone crazy. Breathing hard, I ask, "Why you stop?"

"You said I wasn't getting no ass, so why should I let you get a nut?" He smirks.

"You got me fucked up," I say, tugging at his basketball shorts. Once I get them down and around his ankles, I mount his dick, letting out a soft moan as my body adjusts to him. I start to rock back and forth as he grabs hold of my ass cheeks, matching my pace. After pulling my gown over my head, he tosses it on the side of the couch and wraps his mouth around my pointed nipples. Even though I didn't think it was possible, my pussy gets wetter as he licks and slurps on them like he's trying to feed.

I steady myself by grabbing hold of the back of his neck. Placing a foot on each side of his legs, I start to bounce. Coming all the way up his shaft to the tip of his pole, I tighten my pussy muscles and slowly drop back down. I know that shit drives him wild, and I always aim to please my man.

When he can't take it anymore, he kicks the shorts off from around his ankles and picks me up. Placing me face down on the couch, he enters me once again, from the back this time. From there, he tears my little ass up, and boy does that shit feel good. I look back at him, crying out, loud forgetting my baby is sleep on the next couch. Making sure it doesn't happen again; I bury one of the throw pillows against my face and let it all out.

"How this shit feel?" he asks as he thrusts himself in and out of me.

Panting as he hits my spot repeatedly, I mutter, "Oh shit, it feels good baby….Don't stop."

Gripping my hips tightly, he puts his leg up on the couch and starts to grind. "Whose pussy is this?" he asks.

"This yo' pussy, baby; get this pussy." We switch positions and I'm riding him in a backwards cowgirl as he sits back on the couch moaning and groaning. Reaching down between my legs, I work the shit out of my clit with two fingers as I bounce up and down. I know he's about to cum when I feel his dick pulsating, so I speed up the pace, bringing myself to an orgasm. "I knew you couldn't live without this good shit," he joked. We are still naked on the couch, and he's behind me with his arms wrapped around my waist; we're both exhausted.

"Last time I checked, you came fucking with me and I was minding my own business," I admonish him.

"Say what you want," he counters, "but you know the truth. Just say that you can't get enough."

"I can't get enough," I admit. I lean my head back and tongue-kiss him in the mouth. "You see what I'm saying?" I was a freak and I knew it; I just couldn't get enough of his black ass.

It's Sunday, so I know he's not going anywhere because it's considered "Family Day" for us. It's a habit we started when Raisha was born.

"What do you want to do today?" I ask, getting up from the couch.

"I don't know, boo," he answers lazily. "What do you have in mind?"

"Well, first, I have to take a shower; I feel all sticky and shit," I'm referring to the fluid running down my leg. We never use protection because I'm on The Pill, but I hate to walk around leaking. That shit is so nasty to me, especially when I stand up; it feels like I'm on my period.

By the time we both are out of the shower, Raisha is awake and sitting up in the same spot. After giving her a bath, we lounge around the house for a couple of hours doing nothing in particular. I wasn't in the mood to go anywhere, so we decided on making it a movie night. We all got dressed and went to get some popcorn and take out from Applebee's.

As soon as we're back at the house, I head into the kitchen to prepare our plates while Raimone gets the movie book out. I filled my plate with buffalo wings and fries, while he had a chicken Alfredo and garlic bread. Raisha had spaghetti from the kids' menu and some applesauce. Carrying our trays and her highchair into the living room, I take a seat on the couch as Raimone picks a movie to watch. The first choice is "Baby's Day Out," Raisha's favorite. That girl could laugh so hard at the way the baby was moving throughout the city.

We always let the first movie be about her, because by the time it was over, she'd be out cold. Like always, two hours later, my baby was out for the count, with spaghetti all over her pretty little face. Raimone takes her into the bathroom to wash her up before laying her in her room so that she could sleep comfortably. I gather the trays, the highchair, and clear out the dishes and place them into the dishwasher. When I am done I go back into the living room and stretch out on the couch.

Smacking me on my ass with the palm of his hand, he says, "Scoot yo' ass over!"

I smile and sit up straight. "I was waiting on you to come back."

"What you wanna watch?" he asks.

"Training Day," I answer predictably.

Shaking his head, he says, "I don't even know why I ask."

I don't know why either, because that was always my choice. That was my mutha'fuckin movie! Oh how I love Denzel's fine ass! He played the shit out of that part, and my panties got wetter with ever word he spoke.

The movie eventually ended and I was still amped, even though I had to go to work in the morning. I'm not sleepy and neither is Raimone. Using the remote to turn off the DVD player and TV, he picks me up and carries me back into our bedroom. We take a shower together and from there we continue where we left off earlier. I'm so exhausted by the time we finish, and I can barely keep my eyes open. Snuggling up under my husband, I fall asleep with a smile on my face, not knowing that tomorrow he'd be my worst enemy.

♛ ♛ ♛ ♛ ♛ ♛ ♛ ♛ ♛ ♛ ♛ ♛ ♛ ♛ ♛ ♛

Raimone

I roll over in the bed at around 10 o'clock Monday morning, only to find Sasha's side empty. She's at work, and Raisha was more than likely with her grandparents. With my eyes still closed, I reminisce about how good she made me feel last night when I was inside her. Her skin felt like silk and it was as if she had me in a trance as I touched every part of her body; I just couldn't get enough! Opening my eyes, I wait for a minute to allow them to adjust to the brightness of the room before I go to the bathroom to relieve my bladder.

It takes me all of an hour to take a shower and prepare myself for the day ahead. After I'm finished getting dressed, my phone beeps loudly to notify me that I have a voicemail: Naitaisha's. I know she's probably pissed because the message was from two days ago. She was calling to ask me when I was coming through to see her and my daughter, which would probably be tonight. I don't know what it is about that girl that keeps me coming back, other than my child. I have to admit some I have type of feeling for her; and as long as will she allow me, I'm going to continue to be in her life.

Don't get me wrong, I know that it's fucked up how I'm playing my hand, but as long as I don't get caught there's nothing wrong with it, right? I tell Taisha that I love her all of the time, and I also tell her that when I get everything wrapped up with Sasha, I'm gonna leave my wife. Honestly that couldn't be further from the truth. I could never see myself with Taisha like that. She's not even girlfriend material, let alone wife material. She's a beautiful girl and all, but I need a partner with a goal or a plan as to what she is going to do with her future. All Taisha wants to do is spend money, drink, fuck, or club hop with her busted-ass friends. That may be cool for the next nigga; but for a polished nigga like me, that ain't gonna cut it.

Truthfully at this moment, I want both of them. But I know that one day I'm gonna have to cut Taisha off, because leaving Sasha is not an option. Tashia is cool, but Sasha is my air and everybody knows that you can't survive without air. We've grown together from teenagers to adults and I can't see her with anyone other than me. If I had a chance to alter Sasha in any way, I wouldn't change a thing because to me, she's perfect! When she smiles the room brightens; and when I see her and Raisha interact, I love her even more; she's a great mother. While Taisha, on the other hand, leaves Moni with her mother every chance she gets.

I know you're probably thinking that if I feel so strongly about Sasha, why am I cheating? I really can't answer that question because frankly I don't even have a clue myself. Most men cheat because of something they are missing at home, but that's not my case at all. My wife is the total package: she's independent, beautiful, cooks, cleans, handles my money, takes care of our daughter, and she's a freak; a man couldn't ask for more. So why am I with Taisha? I don't know the real reason behind it, other than the fact that she allows me to be with her knowing my situation. Like I said before, as long as she allows me to be in her life, that's where I'll be. If shit were to hit the fan, I know that I'd be fucked up; and trust me, I'd leave Taisha's ass without a second thought. Right now though, I'm good, so hey, I'll cross that bridge when I get to it.

Hopefully that won't happen anytime soon, because I cover my tracks pretty well. Sasha works from 9–5 p.m., so while she's at work I have more than enough time to spend with my second family. In my profession there is no time clock, so for all Sasha knows I could be handling business and that's exactly what I lead her to believe. I have a lot of free time on my hands because all I actually do is supply product and pick up cash. As long as I'm home during the evening when Sasha gets off, and on Sunday, we have no problems. Occasionally I make up some excuse as to why I have to run out for a few; but other than that, I give her the quality time she needs.

The only plans I had for Monday was to go see Taisha and Moni, so I didn't need to stunt. I throw on dark blue Rocawear jeans, a white tee, and crisp white Force's. My phone rings as I'm in the mirror looking myself over. Upon hearing "Cater to You" by Destiny's Child, I know that it is Sasha.

"Hey, baby," I speak into the phone.

"Hey, Daddy, what are you doing?" she asks.

"Nothing much, just getting ready to run over to Rob's house to shoot dice," I lied. Rob was my boy, and we did kick it a lot, but today wasn't the day. Sasha knew that if Rob and I were gambling, I'd be gone damn near all night. I didn't play around when it was money on the line, so she wouldn't trip if she called and I didn't answer.

"Oh, well what time should I expect to see you tonight?" she wants to know.

"I'm not sure baby, you know how them niggas get when they got money on the table," I told her, hoping that she didn't push it any further. I hated to lie to her, but I had to do what I had to do.

"Well call me when you get a chance," she says sweetly, "and be careful. You know how men get when they are losing their money. I love you, baby, and I'll see you later on."

"I will, and I love you, too. See you later," I say as we end the call. I think about calling Naitaisha, but figure I'll surprise her by popping up unannounced. After brushing my hair, I look in the mirror at my reflection once more before heading out.

The sun shines in my eyes as I step out of the front door. Walking toward my car, I hit the unlock button on my key ring and then climb into my black-on-black Dodge Charger on 24 inch Lorenzo's. When I stick the key in the ignition, the engine comes alive.

"Shawty crunk on the floor wide open, skeet so much they call her Billy Ocean. Roll like an eighteen wheeler, that hoe fine but this hoe a killer. She leaking, she soakin' wet. She leakin, soakin' wet. Shake it like a salt shaker...."

Bobbing my head to "Shake It Like a Salt Shaker" by the Ying Yang Twins, I pull out of the driveway headed toward the freeway. Halfway there I feel my phone vibrating in my pocket; it's Taisha, so I decide to fuck with her a little bit.

Turning down the radio, I nonchalantly ask, "What's up?"

"What's up?" she responds. "What the hell you mean what's up! I left yo' ass a message the night before last and you ain't call me back, and now you want to answer, talking about some what's up!" She was heated and I loved every minute of it.

"Look, girl. I ain't got time for this shit!" I toy with her.

"Who the fuck are you talking to?" she demands. "What, you around yo' girl or something?"

"Don't worry 'bout all of that, I'm kinda busy right now," I claim. "I'll call you when I get a chance, just wait by the phone."

"Muthafuck" was all I heard before I disconnected the call. I hit the power button, turning off my phone, all the while laughing my ass off because I know she's pissed that I'd just hung up on her.

I pull up in the driveway, then I quickly get out of the car while searching for my house key. Once I find the one I'm looking for, I stick it into the lock and walk in. I could hear her upstairs in the bedroom, going off on the phone, talking to one of her nosy-ass friends, either Ti Ti or Big Pat's fat ass. Creeping up the stairs slowly, I try to make as little noise as possible so that she doesn't hear me. She's standing with her back to me with a pair of hot pink boy shorts that say "Whatever" on the back and a white wife beater. I can see the bottom of her ass cheeks, and my dick is getting hard at just the sight. "Girl, I can't wait until he calls, I'm gone cuss his ass out. That muthafucka hung up on me, and turned his phone off. You should've heard the way he was carrying me, like I was some kinda lame bitch or something! The nigga even told me to wait by the phone, so you know I'm pissed!" She must have been mad, because she was pacing back and forth, ass jiggling with every step. She only paces when she wants to stop herself from going over the edge. Her back is still towards me as I slowly walk up behind her and place my arms around her waist, scaring the shit out of her.

"What the fuck?" she screams as her body jerks. Relieved to see that it was just me, she quickly told whoever was on the phone that she would call her back.

"I should fuck you up for the way you played me earlier." She says, dropping the phone and striking me in the chest with her fist. "You're lucky I didn't know where you were, or else I would've found you and kicked yo' ass!"

I was laughing, while at the same time I was holding her arms to stop her from hitting me again. While she's trying to pull her arms free from my grasp, I lean forward and place a soft kiss on her lips.

"What happened?" I ask, running my finger over one of the numerous scratches on her face.

"Some hating-ass bitch at the bar. Don't worry babe, I served her ass just right," she assures me with a sneaky smirk, while avoiding my gaze; she's always into shit!

"Where's Moni?" I ask, irritated. If she stayed her ass out the bar, she wouldn't be fighting every other weekend.

"Taking a nap. She'll be up shortly," she replies, breathing heavy. My irritation instantly goes away; this is my cue to get some before the child wakes up. I guess Taisha had the same plans, 'cause before I knew it, her arms were around my neck, and she's wrapping her legs around my waist. Carrying her over to the king-size sleigh bed, I place her on her back.

Exploring her mouth with my tongue, I grip her soft, round ass. She responds by wrapping her legs around me tighter and grinding slowly. My dick jumps when I feel how moist she is through the thin fabric of her boy shorts.

She throws her head back and moans as I pull her wife beater up and suck softly on her nipples. Pushing me back gently, she slowly pulls the wife beater the rest of the way over her head. After slithering out of her boy shorts, she kicks them at me, and then she lays back on her elbows, slowly fingering her love button. It drives me wild when she does that shit, and she knows it. I undressed quickly while looking at her nice shaved pussy, thinking about how good it's going to feel when

I get inside.

Gripping her by her legs, I pull her down toward the end of the bed and place my face in between her thighs, tasting her juices. She moans loudly as I attack her clit with a vengeance. Once she starts to shake and shudder, I know it is a wrap. Her legs lock around my head as she cums hard in my mouth. I don't mind; I just lap up every drop. Once she lets me loose from the death grip she has on my head, she pulls me up and sucks her juices off of my tongue.

"Tastes like candy," she says, running her tongue across my lips and laying me on my back.

I let out a gasp because in one quick motion she makes my dick disappear in her mouth. Looking me in my eyes she bobs up and down on my shit like she was in a dick-sucking contest.

When I feel myself getting ready to bust I attempt to push her away, only to get my hand smacked. My toes curl and I cry out like a bitch as she continues at a faster pace until I erupt like there's no tomorrow. I watch in amazement as she drinks everything I give her, licking her lips when she's done. Boy she does know how to please her man! If it was only all about fucking, she would make any man proud; but it was deeper than that. There were some men in this world who would be content with a woman who didn't want to do anything but please her man. To each his own! That's cool if that's what they like. I, on the other hand, wanted someone with a good head on her shoulders, not just someone who gave "good head," and Taisha wasn't that person.

Placing my dick back into her mouth, she slowly and softly sucks on it until it's hard once again.

"Do you wanna fuck me, or shall I fuck you?" she

offers, while moving up my body like a feline. Putting my hands on her small waist, I answer her question by pushing her down so that I can work my manhood inside her.

"Damn this shit wet," I exclaim.

"Only for you, baby." She bucks on top of me like she's in a rodeo. All I can do is grip her ass cheeks and enjoy the ride. After forty-five minutes of straight fucking in every position imaginable, we are both spent and tired as hell; I can barely keep my eyes open.

"Daddy!" is all I hear as Taisha jumps up, scrambling to retrieve the covers that were thrown all over the bed to conceal both our naked bodies.

"Hey, Moni," I said through sleepy eyes.

"Daddy, are you sleepy?" she questions with that little girl voice.

"I was, but not anymore. Come ova here and give Daddy a kiss on the cheek." I sit up to give her better access. Come on now. You know I couldn't give her a kiss on the lips with her mother's fresh pussy juice on them, now could I? While Taisha's in the hall bath washing Moni up, I jump in the shower and get dressed. Remembering that my phone was off, I reach into my pocket, powering it back on, and put it on vibrate. I play with Moni downstairs while Taisha's in the shower, and about thirty minutes later we are ready to go.

I end up spending the day like I promised, with Taisha and Moni. We went shopping for toys and clothes, and I made sure that they had everything that they needed. I took Moni to Toys "R" Us and bought her some toys, and a couple of Dora movies. Then we went to Beachwood Mall, where I spent about five stacks making sure that my ladies were happy. Right now we're pulling into the driveway after stopping at Boston Market for dinner.

"Are you staying here with us tonight, Mone?" Taisha whines after we unload everything out of the trunk.

"Tai, you know I can't do that," I say, agitated, as I grab the last bag.

"How long do you expect me to be fine with this part-time shit?" Her hands are on her hips and she's looking teary-eyed. I roll my eyes up into my head, preparing for the bullshit; it never fails.

"Look, Tai, you knew what you signed up for in the beginning. You said you were fine with it, so what's the problem now?" I ask, getting tired of this damn conversation. Shit, we have it at least once a week.

"The problem is, I ain't fucking with nobody else, trying to be true to you! But for what? What do I get in exchange? A wet ass, a couple of dollars, and a lot of cum in my belly? Do you even love me?" she cried.

You see, this is why she could never be my woman. What polished woman you know would say some nasty shit like that?

I respond back, "You know I do, but—"

"But what?" she continues, although it's futile. "Why can't we be a family? What does she have that I don't? Why can't I have you all to myself? Your daughter needs you too. What do you expect me to do? I get tired of sitting here lonely at night while you're at home being a family man to your other family." Her voice whined higher. "I want a man to hold me at night, but I have to sit here alone. I want to be able to go out together and not have to go to another city, just so you won't get busted!"

At that point, she went into a long monologue of the same old stuff: "Moni asks about you daily, and I'm stuck here lying to her like always. I tell her you'll be here soon, when I'm not sure when the hell I'll see you again. I'm not going to keep putting me or my daughter through this. I want a full-time man, this part-time shit ain't for me. You're right. I did sign up for this, because at the time I had no choice. But you're not going to act like you're the victim here, because I came into this situation blind, when you had motives. I've never deceived you. I'm nothing but true and this is how you repay me? If I'm not what you want, let me go. You're married and you keep telling me that you going to leave her, but that time never comes!" She started outright bawling. "So I ask you again, Raimone, what do you expect me to do?"

In response, I start by telling her that she'll never have me all to herself. I want to say also that she could never be half the woman that Sasha is, but I keep that to myself. "I feel ya, Tai, trust me I do. I'm wrong to ask you to commit to a nigga who is with someone else. I will try to give you and Moni more of my time, but I just can't up and leave Sasha right now; I got too much invested in that."

I delve deeper into lies. "If I divorce her now, she'll take everything away from me, including my Raisha, and I can't have that. Just give me some more time, and I promise I'll make it up to you. I'm not feeling her any more and I haven't been for a long time. Baby, we don't even sleep in the same bed, so you know we don't have sex." I stated this with a straight face. In fact I was never leaving Sasha, and if Taisha really believed that lie, she was a damn fool!

"I hope so," Taisha says. "I'm just saying, don't play with my feelings, if this is not where you wanna be.

I love you a lot, but if this is not going to work, you need to let me go. If you continue to hurt me, there's no telling what I might do." It was with this last threat that she walked into the kitchen to prepare our plates.

We watch one of the Dora DVDs that I bought for Moni, and afterwards I bath her and put her to bed. Tai is quiet the whole time, and I know that I have to do something soon because I can tell that she's really getting tired of my bullshit. I walk into the bedroom, take off my shirt, and sit on the bed.

"What are you doing," she says, waving her hand. "I ain't giving you no pussy."

I scoot closer toward her. "I don't want no pussy girl, I'm staying the night with my babies." She smiles brightly and leans in to plant a kiss on my lips.

"So you don't want no pussy, huh?" she says mockingly.

Licking my lips, I protest, "Hey, if you wanna give me some, I ain't gone turn it down."

Jumping up and heading towards the bathroom, she looks over her shoulder. "Take a shower with me," she beckons. By the time I hear the shower water come on, I'm completely naked.

Once inside the shower, Taisha gently washes my body as if I were a baby. I then return the favor. As she drops to her knees to orally please me, the water runs through her hair. All I can do is throw my head back and moan, 'cause the shit felt so good. When I can't take it anymore, I pick her up and turn her around so that I can eat her pussy from the back. In no time I have her cumming like a faucet, as I position my dick on the outside of her wetness and push myself in. The water beats down on my back as I plunge in and out of her. The last thing I remember is her laying on my chest back in the bed, as I let sleep take over.

I should've taken my ass home.

Chapter Five

Naitaisha

Boy, do I love this man; I can't wait until this is permanent. Moni is sleeping, and I am so fucking satisfied. I'm sitting here watching him sleep, as if he were a baby. Well he is…my baby.

Buzzzzzzz buzzzzzzzz is all I hear. Thinking that it's my phone, I sit up in the bed. I was preparing to get up until I realize that my phone is in my purse downstairs. It vibrates again, and I slide my nosey ass out the bed, grabbing my robe off of the chair and walk over in the direction of the noise. It's Raimone's phone and it's inside his jeans pocket. I want to get it so bad but I'm scared that he's gonna catch me. Tying the robe I slowly tip-toe over to the bed and stand there as I listen to him snore lightly, letting me know that he's in a deep sleep. After standing for a few seconds, I go back over to his pants and even though I've never touched his phone before, I reach inside and pull it out. It's 3 a.m. I know that nobody else is calling but that bitch Sasha; tonight I got something for her ass! I glance over my shoulder toward the bed to make sure he's still knocked out, and take the phone with me to the downstairs bathroom.

Taking the stairs quietly, I move at a quick pace because I'm ready to burst this bitch's bubble real hard. My feet are cold on the kitchen tile, and I'm pissed at myself for not putting on my house shoes before I came down. After closing the bathroom door, I lock it and sit on top of the closed toilet bowl, preparing to do damage. As soon as I flip the phone open, I read where it says, "Three missed calls." Pressing the View key, my suspicions are correct because it says Home. Because I'm already on the phone, I go to his contact list to see what name he has my number stored under, and I'm mad as fuck when I see that it's under Tay. Ain't this 'bout a bitch? This nigga got my name spelled as if I'm one of his niggas or some shit! He know damn well I spell my name with an I, not a fucking Y, so why he playing the fuck outta crazy is beyond me!

Because I can't take my anger out on him right now, I'm going for the next best thing. Once I get back to the missed calls screen, I press the Send key to call this hoe back.

"Hey baby," she says, and I can tell she's smiling through the phone. It turns my stomach to hear her call him baby, even though it's me on the phone.

"Who is this?" I ask, knowing that I just wiped the smile right off her ugly ass face.

"Who is this?" she stammers.

"You called this phone," I state coldly. "Is there someone in particular you would like to speak to?"

"Uh yeah, I would like to speak to my husband Raimone," she yells, "And who the fuck are you?" She's so loud that I have to jerk the phone away from my ear temporarily.

"No need to get feisty, sweetie. Mone is busy right now, so he's gonna have to get back with you a little bit later." I'm trying not to laugh, because I know I just broke her fucking heart.

"Look bitch! I don't know who you are or what kind of game you're playing, but you need to get Raimone on the phone." Sasha barreled on, "I ain't with this childish shit. I'm too grown for this here. I'm seriously trying not to get out of my hook up, but you're making it hard by taking it there. Now I'm going to ask you again to put Raimone on the phone, or I will find out who you are and beat the breaks off yo' ass" she tells promises me, and I can hear a viper hiss like she's talking through clenched teeth.

"You look bitch," I let her have it. "I ain't the one playing games, and I ain't trying to hear that dumb shit you talking. So honestly, you can save all that non-sense for the next bitch, because I definately ain't worried about getting my ass beat by yo' bum ass!" I continued, evilly, "You called this mutha'fuckin phone while I'm over here tryin' to get some dick, and now you screaming all in my ear. I should be the one mad and yelling in yo' ear, cause you fucking up my groove. What the hell yo' bored ass want anyway at three in the damn morning? Mone is sleeping off his first nut, and I'm patiently waiting on him to wake up so that he can long-dick me again. So like I told you a minute ago, he's gonna have to get with you another time, 'cause right now I'm 'bout to get my pussy ate," I say as I quickly close the phone.

After I erase my call to her from the call log, I power the phone off and slide to the floor, cracking up. Tears are rolling down my face as I laugh the hardest I've laughed in a long while. My stomach is hurting and I have to put my hand over my mouth to muffle the sound so that my chuckles cannot be heard throughout the house. You just don't know how I wish that I could be a fly on the wall when he goes home. I know it's going to be some shit, 'cause home girl is pissed!

After a few minutes I finally stand up and get myself together by grabbing a couple pieces of tissue and dabbing the tears off of my face. Quietly I walk back up the stairs and into my bedroom, happy that Raimone is still sleeping soundly. After I put the phone back in the exact same place, I stroll over to my side of the bed, dropping the robe onto the floor. I get under the covers naked and snuggle up under my man, putting my titties up against his back. You couldn't take the smile off my face if you tried.

My heart is beating fast and I'm feeling high. I know for sure I won't be able to fall asleep any time soon, because I'm so excited. Looking over at Raimone, I roll onto my back, lick two fingers, and slide them down between my legs. Moaning, I continue to play with my clit as I slide a few fingers from my other hand into my pussy and rock back and forth. The sensation feels good, but not as good as I need it to feel right now, so I reach into my nightstand and pull out my dildo (I call it Javier) and my pocket rocket. I twist the pocket rocket slightly to check to make sure that the batteries are still good; I'm satisfied when I hear the powerful buzz sound. Placing two pillows on top of each other behind me, I prop myself up and pull my legs up, bending them at the knee. Gliding Javier to the back of my throat, I suck on it until it's nice and wet before I slide it into my special spot. Moving it inside me at a rapid pace, I place the rocket directly on my clit and in a matter of minutes I'm cumming like no tomorrow.

"Shit," I pant heavily, trying to catch my breath and enjoying the sensation.

I lay in bed thinking about how life is going to be so wonderful with Mone here every day. I deserve to be Mrs. Raimone Ford, not that broken-down bitch! Yeah, her world is about to come crashing down, and I want to be the one to make it happen. She isn't worthy of him, and I don't understand why she just won't let him go when she knows that he doesn't want to be with her. If I lived under the same roof as my husband and we slept in separate bedrooms and had no sex, I would leave his ass in no time! I guess some people just hold on to whatever they can, even if they only get the bare minimum. It's pathetic if you ask me, because I wouldn't deal with shit like that. I suppress a giggle thinking about how pitiful Sasha is, as I drift off into sleep with my man beside me.

Chapter Six

Sasha

I realize I'm screaming and hollering at the top of my lungs to no fucking body when I hear the operator telling me to hang up and try my call again. After pressing the End button on the phone, I pace back and forth before I hit Redial. The voicemail is coming straight on so I know that either Raimone, or whoever the bitch was, turned the phone off. I'm livid right now and I could kill him and that bitch. I sling the phone across the room, causing it to hit the wall and break in half before it falls to the floor. He knows that I don't play these little kid-ass games, what the fuck is he thinking? Having these hoes call my house from his phone, what part of the game is that?

It's been two hours and neither Raimone nor has his lil bitch has called or said anything. I've been through every emotion there is from sad, to mad, to being worried about his safety. Call me crazy or even stupid if you want, but he has never disrespected me in any way, so I'm wondering: why now? I don't know if that is with him for real, or if something has happened to him while he was gambling and someone has his phone. I've dialed his number about a thousand times from my cell phone, and I still received no answer. Then I have an idea. It's crazy because I don't know why I didn't think of it sooner. I'm going to drive over to Rob's house and see what the fuck is going on.

It's a good thing I let Raisha stay the night over my parent's house, or I'd just be stuck in this bitch. There is no way in hell that I'd be taking my baby out of the house at no damn five in the morning to chase after no fucking body! I hate it when desperate bitches chase after their men with the kids in the car; how pathetic is that? These hoes be riding all over the city looking for a nigga for hours at a time. Babies crying in the back seat and shit and the dumb-ass momma's yelling to them to "Shut up!" like it's the damn kid's fault she picked a loser. Shit don't make no sense, if you ask me.

I throw on a Rocawear jogging outfit, pull my hair into a tight ponytail and slide on some Pumas. I make sure that the Glock that Raimone bought me is secure inside my purse and grab my keys. I'm out the door in three minutes flat. It takes me thirty minutes to pull up at Rob's house and I'm shocked when I see that it appears that all the lights are out. I jump out of the car with my purse right by my side. You never know what the fuck you might walk into, so I wanted to have my gun ready for action. I ain't no killer, but I'll bust a cap in somebody's ass if she fucks with what's mine! After ringing the door bell, it takes Rob maybe two minutes to open it and I can tell he had been asleep.

"Hey, Rob, is Raimone here?" I ask, rocking back and forth. At this point I know damn well he's not.

"Naw, Sasha, I ain't seen the nigga all day," he said sleepily. "I actually just got in myself. I got back from Chicago a couple hours ago," he tells me, rubbing his eyes with the back of his hand. I guess my face says it all because he asks, "What's wrong? When was the last time you spoke to him?"

"Well I talked to him earlier, and he said that he was coming over here to gamble with you. Around three in the morning I call his phone a couple times but he doesn't answer. I figure he's here shooting dice, so I don't call back. As I'm about to get in the bed, my house phone rings. Seeing his number in the caller ID, I quickly answer all sweet and shit, but to my surprise it's a bitch. She told me that Raimone was busy and that he'd call me later. Of course you know I flip on this hoe. She then starts to tell me that she's waiting on him to wake up from his first nut, woopty woo, woopty woo, and then hangs up the phone. I continue to call his phone, but it's turned off." I can't help but cry as I tell Rob the story. I realize clearly that because Raimone isn't at Rob's house like I thought, then Raimone of course is somewhere else. I mean, why else would he lie to me about where he would be?

"Calm down, Sasha," Rob said comfortingly. "It's going to be all right. Maybe he lost his phone. I'm sure he's okay; he's probably on his way home as we speak," he says to me in a tone like I'm a fucking idiot.

"Maybe you're right," I tell him, just so I can go on about my business. I bid Rob farewell and jump on the highway headed home. Just as I suspected, Raimone is nowhere to be found, but I'm not worried because I got something for his ass.

I call Tasha and give her the 411 on what went down, and just like I thought she was ready to ride on him and his lil bitch. I calm her down and tell her that I will come over later when I pick up Raisha. I had something for Raimone's ass. I don't have to deal with this shit. He doesn't know who he's fucking with—I betcha that!

I wrap my hair, take a nice long bath and rub vanilla body oil on my body. I then head to my closet and pick out my work outfit, deciding to wear my blue scrub top with light pink hearts all over it and my blue bottoms. Finishing my outfit off, I choose a light pink, warm-up scrub jacket and pink cotton clogs. After laying them on top of the chair inside my bedroom, I quietly collect my thoughts.

Raimone makes a whole lot more money than I do, with his illegal activities. But I can hold my own if need be. I've been at my job for the past three years, have a Bachelor's degree, and I make $35 an hour. Because I don't have to spend my own money, I put all of my paychecks and a lot of the money that he gives me into the bank. So it's safe to say that I have more than enough to take care of myself and Raisha if I have to. I'm my own woman, far from a needy bitch! I make my own money and I can take care of myself. I'm going to show him that shit today, and he'll see exactly what the hell I mean!

At five o'clock sharp I leave work and head to my car, prepared to pick up my baby. Tasha had an early day today, so she went and picked up Raisha from our parents' house. They were waiting on me at her house. I had in mind a two-week vacation, which I planned on spending with my daughter.

Raimone has been calling my phone all day; but guess what: Fuck him! I'm thinking he finally showed up at around 10 a.m., because that's when the calls started. I had to sit up and wait on his ass all fucking night, wondering if every single noise I heard was him coming in the house; which never happened.

No sooner had I opened up the door to walk into Tasha's condo, but my baby girl is running full speed at me. "Mommy, Mommy!" she yells as she jumps into my arms. I smoother her cheeks with kiss after kiss. Tasha comes around the corner with a scarf on her head, looking as if she's ready to go to war.

"What's up big sis?" she asks, slightly leaning against the wall. She always calls me that because I was born three minutes before she was.

"Nothing much," I replied. "I just started a two-week vacation from work and I'm ready to relax. I'm about to check in at the Towne Place Suites, not far from here."

"Why are you going there?" she asked. "You know you can stay here as long as you like. Shit, I got more than enough room for you and Rai-Rai," she tells me, referring to her condo in Westlake.

"I know that, Tash," I nod, "but I really want to get away. Plus you know this is the first place he's gonna check. I've already paid for my room for the whole two weeks, and my car is packed up with our clothes."

"So you really gonna leave him?" She added, "I mean, I'd fuck him up if I were you; but leave him? No. I'll even help you, but that's your husband and he takes care of home. He's also the best father I've ever seen, besides Daddy. Just think about what you're going to do before you fly off the deep end like you usually do. You know how you are sometimes, so will you do that for me, Sash?" she asks, looking concerned. She knew more than anybody that sometimes I was one to not think about my actions.

"Honestly, I don't know what I'm going to do; I just need some time to myself. Even if I do go back, he'll know that I'm a force to be reckoned with," I tell her with a smile. She goes on to tell me that whenever I need "Me" time to let her know, and she'll keep Raisha. I tell her I'll let her know, but I do looking forward to spending time with my baby, doing girly things. I thank her, and tell her that if Raimone calls, for her to tell him that I came to get Raisha and that she doesn't know where I am. I inform her that my phone will be off for most of the day, so to leave a message if she needs me, or call the hotel to be transferred to my room.

After stopping at Burger King to get us something to eat, Raisha and I head to the hotel. I unload the trunk that contains our rolling suitcases, and lug them inside. We check in after I receive my key card, and we are on our way up to room 224. The room I paid for was a two-bedroom suite, equipped with two queen-size beds, a living room, and a full-size kitchen. I have to remember to go to the grocery store tomorrow to pick up a few things. At around ten, Raisha is sleeping while I sit on the couch watching "Bad Boys."

"Let me cater to you, cause baby this is your day" plays from my cell phone.

Damn, I say to myself. I meant to turn my phone off, but I forgot and now Raimone is calling again. Once again I ignore his shit. I have plans for the next week or so. I also gotta remember to change his ringtone to That's Just My Baby Daddy by B-Roc and The Biz. Hey, I know I'm petty, but who gives a damn! I call Tasha to let her know that we made it safely, and she tells me that Raimone has called her constantly, telling her that he's worried and that he wants me to call him immediately. I tell her to tell him to go fuck himself, and that I ain't thinking about his ass. We share "I love you's" and hang up. I don't really care if he's worried or not. Did he give a fuck when I was worried last night? Nope, I don't think so. He thinks this is a fucking game? Well, let's play ball!

Chapter Seven

Raimone

"What the fuck is up with Sasha, man?" I yell as I punch the wall. I'm just getting off the phone with Tasha, and what she told me didn't sit well with me. Supposedly, Sasha packed up and took Raisha with her, and they ain't coming back. I am so confused right now; I don't know what the fuck is going on or what to do. I noticed that some of her clothes are missing from the open drawers in our bedroom. I think she left them slightly open so that I could see that she had left. My phone vibrates inside my pocket, and I reach in to answer it, hoping to God that it's Sasha.

"Hello," I answer.

"What's up, playboy?" Rob jokes.

"Shit, man, going through it," I say. "I just got off

the phone with Tasha and she told me that Sash told me to go fuck myself, and that she wasn't thinking 'bout me."

"Damn, man, so she found out, huh?" he asked me, and I don't know what the hell he's talking about.

"Found out what?" I say incredulously.

"That you was ova Naitaisha's, nigga, that's what!" he yells.

"What the fuck you talking about Rob? How the fuck would she find out that?" I asked. I'm getting irritated; I'm pacing back and forth across the living room floor as I wait for his response.

"Look, dude. Sasha came by here last night looking for you, saying something about us gambling. She was worried about you, 'cause some bitch called her from your phone telling her some crazy shit. I guess she thought that somebody had yo' ass tied up or something; she had her strap and all man. I know this because she was clutching that purse like a muthafucka!" he said, laughing.

Clutching her purse? I ain't finding that shit funny at all.

"Man, get the fuck outta here," I exclaim.

"I swear on my momma, nigga," Rob says. "I bullshit you not. I told her you was fine, and to head on home." Rob continues, "You're a dumb bastard, I tell you! Why the hell you ain't call and tell me what the fuck was up? I'm standing here looking like a dumb ass talking to your wife, trying to explain for yo' ass! I've told you time and time again to not put me in that shit! You got you a good girl on your hands. Keep it up and it's a wrap, playboy" he warns me. I already know that he's speaking nothing but the truth. Unfortunately, I ain't trying to hear that shit right now. All I'm thinking about is what the hell I'm going to do to make this right.

"Aight, man, let me handle this," I tell him and close my phone. Now my mind was racing because I don't know what the fuck to do. When did Taisha have time to call her and say anything? Now I see what the fuck is up. No wonder why my cell was off this morning when I woke up. At first I thought it might of died, but when I turned it on I had two notches on the battery. I can't believe Taisha's ole grimey ass, but I'm gonna handle her later.

Right away I gotta try to make it right with my baby. I'm on my way to do just that, but unfortunately for me her phone is off, and the voicemail comes straight on: "Hey, you've reached Sasha, as you can see I'm unavailable at this time. Your call is very important to me, so if you would please leave your info after the beep, I call you back at my earliest convenience. Beeeeep!"

"Hey baby, it's me, I don't know what's going on, but you need to call me as soon as you get this. I talked to Tasha and I'm confused. I don't know what's wrong with you, or why you're not answering any of my calls. Whatever it is, please call and let me know at least that you're okay. We need to talk about whatever it is that's got you so upset. I love you Sash. Bye," I add before I disconnect the call. By now it's damn near 2 a.m., and I know for sure that she isn't coming home tonight. That's good, because I got shit I gotta handle, starting with the slick bitch that caused all of this bullshit.

On my way to Taisha's house I get a call from Mike telling me that he's out of work. Mike is one of my workers who runs the block off of West 65th in Denison; he's a pretty cool dude. Pulling up in front of a rundown house, he opens up the door and climbs in. Mike is what some would call a "pretty nigga" with his light skin and curly hair. He kinda puts you in the mind of Christopher Williams, except for the hazel eyes. But it would be a mistake to let the way he looks fool you, because he is a nigga who will not play. That was one of the reasons why I put him in charge of this block, because I knew that he'd put everyone right where they need to be.

"What's up, Mone?" he says, closing the door.

Once the interior light goes out, I place my focus on a fiend who's walking aimlessly down the street. "Shit, what it look like out here?"

He handed me a roll of money. "Pretty good, if I say so myself."

I scroll through it quickly before opening my glove compartment and throwing in inside. "It's in the truck," I tell him, popping the trunk. He gets out, walks to the rear of my car and disappears; I pull off, headed to my next destination. It's 2:30 by the time I make it across town to Naitaisha's house, so I know that Moni would be sleeping. I jump out of my car, and slowly creep up to the house to unlock the door. All of the lights are off inside the house except for Taisha's, which has the glow from the TV. As I round the corner, I faintly hear the shower running, so of course that is my next destination. I scare the shit outta her when I pull back the shower curtains and just stare at her.

"Ah, shit, Mone, what the hell is wrong with you?" she asks, holding her chest, breathing fast. I just stare at her ass, not saying anything. "Hellooooo Mone, what the fuck is wrong with you?" she asks again, waving her hand in front of my face. This time I just walk out of the bathroom and take a seat on the bed. A few moments later, she walks out of the bathroom dripping wet with a small towel wrapped around her body. Any other time I'd be ready to fuck, but today I was here for something else.

"Why did you do that stupid shit, Taisha?" I ask her through gritted teeth.

"Do what, Mone?" She began drying the water off of her body. She was looking so innocent, and I would believe it if I didn't know for sure she did it.

"Come on, don't play me for dumb," I implored. "Why the hell did you call Sasha last night hollin'?" She lets out a breath and walks over to the dresser to grab some lotion.

"I don't know what you stressing for. It ain't like y'all together. Ain't that what you told me?" she asks while sitting on the opposite edge of the bed applying lotion to her legs.

"It don't matter what I tell yo' ass, you ain't have no business calling my wife, you dumb-ass girl! Sasha left me and took my daughter because of the stupid shit you pulled!" I yell as I walk over to where she is.

"Wait a muthafuckin minute, your wife? Are you standing here mad at me, because you can't keep yo dick in yo pants?" She pointed down between my legs. "Don't make your bed if you can't lay in it, BITCH! Fuck Sasha. What about me?"

"What about you? Taisha, don't play yo' self; we are talking about my family here," I say calmly because I don't want to wake up Moni.

"Your family? Is that what you said to me? Moni and I are your family, too, Bitch, or did you forget that? Don't sit here and play like you're the victim here, Raimone. You put yourself in this predicament, not me!

You married that bitch, so you owe her an explanation. I sure as hell don't. I admit I was wrong for touching your phone, but this situation is not my fault. Take responsibility for your own actions, and admit when you're wrong. I'm not going to keep playing second-fiddle to that bitch and her baby— Fuck—" was all she got to say before I smacked the shit outta her. She would've fallen on the bed, but I wrap my hands tightly around her neck to stop her.

I apply pressure, and she was scratching and kicking to get me off of her, but she was no match for my anger. I throw her with all of my might, and her head makes a loud thud as it bounces off of the wall. I'm so angry that I walk over to where she's laying and proceed to choke her once more, showing her no mercy. When I see that she may pass out, I let her fall, and she grabs hold of her neck, gasping. By now the towel she had on is only a distant memory, as she gets up to run to the dresser. I know immediately she's heading for some type of weapon, more than likely a knife.

"Bitch, get the fuck out of my house!" she orders me, holding a big-ass knife in her hand. When she sees that I am not moving, she repeats it. "I said get the fuck out now, before I call the police and put your black ass in jail." By the look in her eyes I know that she's serious. I slowly back out of the room, with the fear that she might stab me in the back if I turn around.

Once I'm in my car, I head home, hoping that she doesn't really put the police in our business. I feel bad for putting my hands on her, because I've never been one to strike a woman for any reason; but tonight I lost it. I guess she hit a nerve with what she was saying, and I couldn't take it. She knew she was wrong for the shit she pulled, but it's also my fault because I shouldn't have stayed the night anyways. If I would've taken my ass home, she couldn't have called and said shit to Sasha.

Lying in the bed alone, I can't sleep. I was too worried about what would happen between me and Sasha. I couldn't lose my family; I refused to lose them. I know I fucked up, but I'm a man; we fuck up all the time. She is my wife; no one comes before her, and she knows that. I take care of home and her with no problems. I just need one chance, and I promise I'll make it right. I can't live without Sasha and my Rai Rai. Without them, I am nothing.

I will do anything in my power to get them both back, and I do mean anything. I know what you're thinking, and I'm not going to do anything stupid like that. I just know that I gotta pull all of the stops to make this right. I would never hurt my girls, especially when it's my own dumb-ass fault they left. I don't understand how men kill their wives and families due to the fact that they fucked up the household in the first place. I'm getting teary-eyed right now thinking about my mom. I still have nightmares about how my sick-ass father murdered her in cold blood, right in front of my eyes.

It was Christmas morning in 1988, and I was 7 year old. I was pulled out of a nice dream to the sound of my mom crying. I should've been used to hearing this, but I sat outside her door and silently cried with her anyway, like I've done on numerous nights before. I never understood why women continue to let these men break their hearts when they ain't bringing shit to the table to begin with. Willie Ford was my so-called "father's" name, but that nigga ain't never been no daddy to me, so I called him Willie. He was a fucking bum, he didn't work. Shit, he really didn't do much of anything but sit around the house, with my mom treating him like a king. Even at a young age I knew that my mom didn't have to take the shit that she did from him. She could've had any man she wanted. Why she choose to marry him is beyond me.

Debra Ford was a beautiful woman. She reminded me of Pam Grier, same skin tone. Not only did she have a pretty face, but she was also a brick house. Willie knew that; that was why his poor ass always made his way back home to Momma after he was done doing who knows what. Well this particular day, I guess Mom finally seen the light and was fed up with Willie's disrespectful ways; she was leaving him for good this time.

"Raimone, what are you doing out here crying, baby?" she asked me after she opened her door. I think she expected me to be still sleeping, which of course I wasn't.

"I heard you crying, Mama, and I felt bad for you," was all I could say between muffles.

"Your Mama's alright, baby. Let's get you cleaned up so you can open your presents," she told me as she led me to the bathroom in our small but clean apartment. After brushing my teeth and washing my face, we headed downstairs so that I could tear the gift wrapping off of my many presents. You see, my mom worked nights as a housekeeper for some rich folk on the far West Side. They gave her very nice bonuses every holiday, and they also sent gifts for me. So I had the gifts that they sent, plus the ones that Mom had bought me. I was living large!

I was still smiling after I opened my last gift, I was

so happy. I got the Nintendo that I wanted with Super Mario Bros and Duck Hunt; I also got new clothes, shoes, and a couple He-Man action figures. While Mom and I ate dinner, I just spoke out of the blue: "Mommy, why don't you leave Willie?" I could tell that I caught her off guard with that question, because she just sat shocked for a minute. I know she was probably wondering what I knew about her and Willie, but I wasn't deaf, dumb, or blind. People think that kids don't know what's going on, as if they are too young to comprehend most things. Trust me, those people are sadly mistaken!

"Baby, what do you know about me and yo' daddy's problems?" she asked with a chuckle.

"I know that he hurts you, and that you're always crying over him. I know that you take care of me. You pay for everything. You're a pretty lady. You can get you a better husband," I assured her, as she sat staring at me, wide-eyed.

"Listen, Raimone. I love your father a lot. We are a family. I'm a strong woman. I don't mind doing things myself. I love taking care of my household, making you and your father happy," she told me, smiling.

"I'm sorry, Mommy. I don't want you to be mad at me," I told her, on the verge of crying. I didn't want to overstep my boundaries, but she asked me, so I told her how I felt.

"I'm not mad baby, keep going, I'm listening," she informed me, placing her elbows on the table and resting her face inside her hands. She reminded me of a little kid at story time, waiting for her teacher to start the book of the day. It was cute, though, cause I guess that was her way of letting me know that she was all ears to whatever I had to tell her.

"Willie isn't good for you; he doesn't do anything but hurt you and sit on the couch. It's Christmas and he's not even here. He didn't buy you or me a gift at all. I hate him and I don't want him here with us anymore!" I moaned, and she came over to console me as I wept.

"Listen, baby, mommy's gonna make a deal with you, alright?" She pulled me back just enough so that she could see my reaction. After I nodded, she continued, "I'll pack Willie's bags, so that they'll be ready for him whenever it is that he comes. All I want for you to do is promise me that you'll remember everything you told me when you grow up and have a family of your own. Your wife and kids should be all that you live for. No matter what you do in the street, you should never disrespect you wife, or let anyone else disrespect your wife in any way. A man protects and takes care of his household, and makes sure everything is how it needs to be. Can you promise your momma that?" she asked.

"Yes I can momma, I won't let you down," I promised her as I kissed her on her cheek. I never got a chance to show her that I was the man I promised to be, because that night was the last night she was alive. At around 10 p.m. my mom tucked me into bed and kissed me goodnight. I woke to her yelling and telling Willie to just leave her alone.

"Get out, Willie, I'm not with this anymore!" she yelled over the music. I guess he had turned up.

"Bitch, I ain't going nowhere. This my muthafucking house!" he roared back. By then I had crept out of my bed and slowly transcended down the hall to the steps. I sat down on the 2nd step from the top, and my young eyes watched everything that transpired through the poles of those steps.

"Oh, you getting the hell outta here, or I'll call the police and they'll escort your monkey ass out!" she threatened him.

"If I catch you even thinking about calling the police on me, bitch, I'll kill your hoe ass!" he bellowed drunkenly. His clothes were wrinkled and his words were slurred. Even a blind man could tell he was drunk. I guess Mom didn't care about his threats, because she picked up the phone and dialed 911.

"Yes. I need the police to come and escort my husband off of my premises, he's drunk..." She never got a chance to finish, due to Willie smacking her in the mouth. She touched her lip, and when she saw blood, her shock wore off. She picked up the phone at the base and threw it, hitting Willie square in the face. We had one of those phones that you see in hospitals now, so you know it had to hurt badly.

"Muthafucka, don't you ever put your hands on me!" she screamed as she charged at him swinging wildly. Because he was drunk, her fists were landing every which way she threw them.

He was trying to block her punches, but she was too wild for him. I guess he got tired of trying to hold her at bay, so he reached all the way back and punched her in the face so hard her neck snapped back. My mom fell on the ground, but before she landed she hit her face on the end table and she stayed there motionless. I ran up the stairs to my room to get something to protect her with. Once I came down the stairs, I saw him hovering over her, his hands tightly around her neck.

His back was to me, and the music was still so loud so he didn't hear me walk up behind him. All you could here was a ding sound as my steel bat connected with his head. I didn't stop swinging until he was off of my mom and on the floor. I dropped the bat and ran to my mom to make sure she was alright.

"Mommy, are you okay?" I asked, as I gazed at the cut above her eye.

"Yes baby, I'm fine, thank you," she gasped. I knew something was wrong when her eyes got as big as saucers, but before I got a chance to see what it was, she was pushing me across the room.

"Bang" was all I heard. I looked up in time to see the smoke still coming out of the hole in my momma's head. He killed my momma, the only person that I had in this world. I sat in terror as I watched the blank look in her eyes. She fell face first on the carpet, as blood leak out and covered the floor.

"You lil mutha'fucka," was what Willie said to me as he walked towards me with this look in his eyes that I will never forget. I was terrified and didn't know how I was going to get away from him. Momma was no longer here to protect me. I don't remember what happened next, because suddenly everything went black.

I woke up to see a lady standing over me, taking my blood pressure in the hospital, with IVs everywhere. I tried to sit up but found the pain too unbearable so I stayed exactly where I was. The lady (later I found out she was my nurse) told me to relax and that the doctor would be in to see me shortly. Apparently after Willie killed my mom, he shot me in the chest and then turned the gun on himself. What kind of sick person would try to kill his own son? Your guess is as good as mine.

My grandma Delores picked me up from the hospital, and I lived with her up until she died of a massive heart attack when I was 18.

So you see, I don't have any family other then Sasha and Raisha. That's why I have to do anything in my power to make sure they both return home, where they need to be. That shit with Taisha is a wrap. I've done enough damage so far, and I'm not trying to fuck up any further. I've got my mind made up; even though I know it's easier said then done.

Chapter Eight

Sasha

It's been a week since I've last seen Raimone, and I'm missing him like crazy. I know he did me wrong, but you just can't turn love on and off. He doesn't make it any better by calling nonstop, leaving voicemails saying how much he loves us and misses us. This past week Raisha and I have been to the movies, salon, museums, and everything else you could probably think of. I try to keep myself busy so that I don't think about Raimone, but as soon as she's sleeping he fills my thoughts. My phone alerts me that I have a text message, so I look to see who it's from, and of course it's Raimone: "Baby please call me I losing my mind w/o u & Raisha. I really need 2 tlk 2 u. Can u @ least answer the phone or call me @ least once. I love u!"

I read the message five times, and I slowly wipe away the tears that slowly fall from my eyes. I hate that I love him so much! I decide to call him to see what he has to say for himself. The phone barely rings before I hear him.

"Hey, Baby," he says, as if he ran to answer it.

"Hey," I say to him in a dry tone, even though I'm kinda happy to hear his voice. You know how it is, I still gotta play the role.

"How have you and Raisha been doing?" he asks.

"We've been fine, the question is who have you been doing?" I ask, because I can't hold my tongue any longer. I go in and kiss Raisha on the forehead and gently close her door so that if I need to raise my voice, I won't disturb her sleep.

"What do you mean by that?" he asks, playing dumb.

"Look, Raimone!" I yell. "I'm on this phone to talk, so talk! I don't have time to play fucking games with you. You betta put all your shit out here on the table right now while you have the chance, cause if I hang up this damn phone, you're done!" I'm pissed off now, because I was nice to call, yet he's trying to play me for a fucking dummy. I go into the bathroom and close the door, because I know that eventually Raisha will hear me and wake up to see what is wrong, and I don't want to scare my baby.

"Okay baby, look, I fucked up," he admits.

"How long have you been fucking with her?" I ask through clenched teeth.

"A couple of months," he hesitantly says, and I flip the fuck out.

"What the fuck? Why? All I do is love yo' ass, and you treat me like this? I sat and waited on your ass all night, I even went to Rob's house looking like a fucking fool! I thought something had happened to you, and you laid up with some bitch." I continue furiously, "When we got together, you told me that you would never hurt me. If that were true, I wouldn't be crying on this phone right now. You asked me to marry you. You asked me! If you weren't ready, you shouldn't have did the shit! After all these years I have never cheated on you, and this is how you repay me? Answer me when I'm talking to you muthafucka!" I scream.

"I'm about to be completely honest with you right now, but you gotta let me finish before you start flipping out on me," he warns.

"I ain't gotta do a damn thing," I throw back. "Talk!"

"Her name is Naitaisha. I met her awhile back, she's actually Chino's lil sister."

"Chino, your connect?" I clarify.

"Yeah, I only started messing with her because one day while he was around she made a pass at me," he explains. "When I didn't attempt to talk to her, Chino asked me was something wrong. I made up some bogus story about how I wouldn't feel comfortable being with his sister like that; but actually I wasn't attracted to her at all. She's skinny, has real bad acne and is funny looking, if you ask me," he admitted. "Anyway, he kept insisting that I take her out and show her a good time, because she doesn't know anyone and he's so far away." He kept rambling, "I took her to the movies once and we went out to eat, but even then she paid for everything. She gives me money all the time, so I figured what harm could it do. It was basically a win-win situation to me."

"So how did you end up over her house that night?" I ask.

"Chino uses her house as my re-up spot, so I went over there that night to do that and pick up the fifteen grand that she promised me. When I got there, she told me that she made me dinner and asked me to spend the night with her, but I told her no and was about to head out to Rob's house. She started to rant and rave about how she was going to tell Chino that I was trying to play her, and in turn he wouldn't fuck with me no more," he continues. "I wasn't trying to lose my connect, so I stayed just to she'd shut up. I never slept with her and I didn't even know that she had called you until Rob told me the next day. Sasha," he promises, "it's over because even with all the money she gave me, it's not worth it."

"How do I know that you won't do this again?" I ask and squint at him.

"I promise you, baby, you will never have to worry about this type of shit from me again. I'm a changed man; this past week has driven me insane. I just need for you to come back and make this house a home again. Will you do that for me?" he begs.

"I don't know, Raimone," I sigh. "I mean, I love you. But how am I ever supposed to trust you again?" I turn on the faucet and splash cold water on my face. I look at my reflection in the mirror and just as I had thought, my eyes are all red and puffy.

"It's gonna take time, and I know that. It wouldn't be fair for me to ask you to give me your all again. What I'm asking is that you give me a chance to prove myself to you. I love you, Sash, and without you and Raisha, there is no me," he sobs. Damn, why did he have to get all soft on a bitch?

"Are you sure that there isn't anything else that you want to tell me, Raimone?" I interrogate. "You think long and fucking hard, because I want you to be sure. Is there anything else that I should know? If so, please tell me right now."

"There isn't anything else to it baby, I swear on life," he promises.

"How about you take me and Raisha out to dinner tomorrow, and we can talk some more."

"That would be perfect! Baby, you won't regret taking me back," he says excitedly.

"Hold on, I didn't say shit about taking you back," I inform him. "What I said was we will talk during dinner tomorrow."

"I feel you Sash. What time is good for you?" he asks.

"Seven is a good time; not too early, not too late. I'm gonna go now, I have things to do," I say, knowing damn well I ain't have anything planned. I was gonna lay in the damn bed and watch another movie. He didn't need to know that.

"Okay, well, I'll see you tomorrow, then" he says sadly.

After we hang up, I pour a glass of wine, light a couple of the candles that I bought and run some water for a hot bath. I put vanilla bubble bath into the water and pull out my night clothes. The water feels good against my skin, so good that I let out a soft moan as I submerge my body. I lift my leg up and slowly run my hands from my ankle past my thighs, where they land on my perky breasts. I throw my head back and massage them at a slow pace, pinching my nipples ever so softly. My right hand finds its way down to my special spot and I rub my clit in a circular motion. I keep the left one on my breast as I continue to twist and pinch my nipple. I glide two fingers inside me and rock to an imaginary beat. The sensation feels so good as I move my fingers in and out at a rapid pace. My body starts to tremble and I whimper as I cum with so much force I temporarily lose my breath.

"Shit," I groan as I exhale, remembering that it's been a while since I've had some.

Even though I haven't told Raimone, I know for sure that I will be returning home. I mean, yeah, he fucked up, but it isn't that bad right? He used that bitch to make sure that me and our child were taken care of. Now that I think of it, that's why that bitch was so ready to tell me she was fucking my man, she is a hater, flat out! So yes I'm going to hold on to my good man, cause that's just what he is. Now don't get it twisted, his ass is going to suffer. I'm just glad this isn't really bad. It could've been a lot worse, a whole lot worse.

Chapter Nine

Naitaisha

"I would've cut that bitch, I swear on life!" Big Pat yells.

"Girl, that's the same thing I said." Ti Ti stands up to give Pat a high-five.

We were sitting in my living room drinking shots of Henny and talking about the fight that I had with Raimone. Well not actually a fight, more like me getting choked-slammed, if you ask me. It had been a week since the incident and he has yet to call and apologize, and I'm pissed. Not pissed about the fact that he fucked me up, but about the fact that he can just shut me out without a problem. I've been calling his phone, only to get sent to voicemail. I leave messages, and he doesn't even attempt to call me back. Of course I'm not gonna tell my girls that, because they aren't about to clown my ass!

"Oh trust me I was going to, but that bastard ran up outta here like Kunta-fucking Kinte," I tell them, laughing. I can always count on my bitches. They sure know how to make me feel better, and I love them for it. We've been hanging since we were little girls and nothing has changed.

Big Pat, whose real name is Patricia Jackson, is part of the BBW club (Big Black Women) but you better not tell her that shit! We met years ago in the second grade during an assembly at Tremont Elementary School. Some girl and a couple of her friends were picking with her, I intervened and we been tight ever since. Even though Pat is 5'4" and damn near 200 pounds, she has a really pretty face. She is the color of a dark chocolate bar, and people used to always tell her that she was pretty to be a dark-skinned girl. What the fuck does that mean anyway? Why couldn't she just be pretty period? What did being light or dark have to do with anything? People automatically assume that just because you had light skin that you would be gorgeous. Which is a damn lie, cause I done seen a lot of funny-looking "light skin" people in my life.

That was just the case with Ti Ti, or Tiffany Dean her government. Ti Ti was a red bone, and even though she's my girl she is not a looker. I mean she wasn't butt ugly, but she wasn't what you would call pretty, either. As I said, Pat was overweight; on the other hand, Ti Ti was 5'8" and built like Buffy the Body. That bitch was thick for no damn reason, and that's the reason niggas flocked to her. She was also what you would call flip-floppy, because one minute she'll be cool and the next she hates yo' ass. I told the bitch that she's bi-polar, but she insists that she ain't. I told the bitch that she needs to make a doctor's appointment, because there's medicine for that shit!

We make it our business to go out every weekend, and trust me we party hard. I'm the only one out of the click who has a child, but finding a babysitter is never a problem because my mom watches Moni with no hesitation. My mother Naomi Bolen is the best mom in the world; she raised me on her own. My father, Nathaniel Meeks (who I've never known), left my mother when I was two. It was a struggle for her to take care of me on her own, but somehow she managed. My mom told us that our father left after his wife threatened to divorce him, take everything, and keep him from his other children. So of course, he left and didn't look back, not thinking even once that I was his child also.

She told me that when she met him, he didn't mention that he was married. She assumed he was a single man, her man. He wined, dined, and even seemed happy when she told him that she was pregnant. He then went out and got all brand-new furniture to go in the apartment that he got for her. She didn't have to buy me clothes (or anything for that matter), because he took care of everything. From the crib to the bibs, I supposedly had it all—that was until a little after my second birthday when she received the shock of her life. It's crazy now that I think about it, because that's exactly where I am right at this moment; I guess the cycle continues. Preparing to get me dressed after my bath, she was interrupted by the ringing phone.

"Hello," she answered.

"Who is this?" I imagine that an unknown female asked.

"Who is this?" my mom asked right back, with a slight attitude.

"Look bitch!" I'm sure the other woman said. "I know exactly who you are, and I'm telling you to stay away from my husband!" I could hear her yelling.

"I'm sorry, but I believe you have the wrong number. I don't even know your husband," my mom said calmly, thinking that this is all a misunderstanding.

"That's right, you are sorry!" the woman probably said sarcastically. "I have the right number, my name is Mrs. Meeks, Nathaniel's wife and I want you to…"

"Wife?" my mom cut her off. "He never told me anything about no wife. We have a child together," she informed the caller.

At that point, the other woman probably blurted out the whole story: "Oh yes, I know all about your little bastard, and this ends today. Nathaniel told me about the baby, and how he's been taking care of you with our money. I'm just calling to let you know that whatever you got, keep it! 'Cause as of today, you won't get another dollar." With that, she hung up.

To say my mom was shocked was an understatement. Shit, she was traumatized. My mother never saw my father again and never even heard from him. No phone call, no letter, just a phone call from the wife. I said it before, and I'll say it again: Niggas ain't shit!

I promised myself that wouldn't be me, but I guess the cycle continues. I hate that my mother never found anyone to settle down with, and to this day I have never seen or heard about her being with another man. I guess my father really did a number on her, even though she won't directly admit it. She used to be a show-stopper back when I was younger, but I guess since she's has no one to look good for, she's let herself go. She went from weighing around 145 to about 260 in a few years' time. I feel bad about Moni being over there all the time, but my mom tells me that she's no problem, and that she's always welcome. I'm guessing maybe Moni gives her something to live for, and who am I to take that away from her, right?

"Taisha! Taisha!" Pat yells, breaking me out of my daydream. "Your phone is ringing, girl."

"Hello" I answer, and I'm shocked by the voice I hear: It's Raimone.

"I need to talk to you," he says simply.

"About what?" I inquire back.

"I'll be there in a half," he says, and then hangs up before I get a chance to respond. Now I'm thinking: How in the hell am I going to get these bitches out of here, and freshen up before he arrives?

I end up making up some bullshit story about me having to go to my mom's house to take Moni some Tylenol. By the time they leave, I only had 10 minutes to spare, so I hopped in the shower to prepare myself for his arrival. The doorbell rang just as I was finished getting dressed. I decided I wanted to look sexy, but not look like I was trying too hard. So I threw my hair into a messy ponytail and put on some tight-fitting plaid pajama pants, and a plain wife beater. I looked into the mirror to make sure that the effect was perfect, and ran down the stairs. I swung open the door with a smile, but Raimone kept a straight face.

"Why didn't you use your key?" I asked him with a smile. That smile was quickly replaced with a frown, because he placed the same key that I just mentioned in palm of my hand.

"What the fuck is this about!" I ask.

"I came over here to tell you that I was sorry for putting my hands on you, I had no right." he apologized.

"Okay, I forgive you, Mone and I know I played my hand all wrong. My question is, what is this about?" I ask again, this time dangling the key in the air.

"I'm giving that back to you because you're right, I can't expect you to put your life on hold. Sasha and I are trying to get past this, and I just can't lose her," he tells me, unable to look me in the eyes.

"What!" I yell. "You can't lose her? What the fuck about me, Mone? What about Moni?" I ask.

"I'm going to make sure that Moni is good…"

"Okay, and what about me?" I ask after I cut him off, pointing to myself.

"You're going to have to get a job; you're not my girl anymore, so I'm not going to take care of you. In this envelope there are 5 G's. It's enough to take care of Moni for a month. I'll make sure to get this to you every month. If you spend how you're supposed to, she'll be fine. If not, then that's on you. I'm taking care of my seed, not you," he told me, handing me a white envelope.

"What are you saying, Mone?" I ask in disbelief.

"I'm saying that this is done, but I'm still going to take care of Moni," he answered. "I'll make sure she's straight."

"So you gonna come up in here, give me money, and walk out of my life and your child's life? So she's never going to see you again?" By now tears are streaming down my face and my heart is hurt.

"Come on now, Tai, you did this. You just couldn't leave well enough alone. You had to be a smart ass, and that's the price that you have to pay. I love Moni, you know I do, and I'll always take of her," he declares while standing up to walk towards the door.

"Ok, Mone. I'm sorry, I fucked up. It won't happen again, I give you my word, just don't leave me!" I beg. "I love you, don't you know that?"

"Look, Tai, I gotta go. Take care of yourself," he calmly states and walks out of the door. I slip on some Air Marx and quickly give chase; he's inside his car by the time I make it outside.

"So you just gonna leave me like this? After all the shit we've been through, you gonna leave me like this? I have your child, too, muthafucka!" I yell as I beat on his driver side window. "This isn't because of me. It's your fault. You're a fucking coward, that's what you are, a fucking coward!" I'm shouting, but by now he's slowly backing out of my driveway. "Bitch, this ain't over, you fucked with the wrong one this time!" I threaten, picking rocks off the ground and flinging them at the back of the car.

By now my neighbors are standing on their porches taking it all in, but I don't give a damn because my heart is broken. I slowly trudge my way into my house, and break down crying once I pass the foyer. What the fuck am I going to do? What I am supposed to tell my daughter? I sit by the door for what seems like hours crying, until I have a plan. I'm not going to be like my mother, and go out without a fight. That bitch is not taking him away from me or my child. That bitch will pay for what she's putting me through, if it's the last fucking thing I do!

Chapter Ten

Sasha

I'm awakened around 8 a.m. by Raimone's call, asking where dinner will be tonight. I tell him that I've chosen Red Lobster, because the "Endless Shrimp" special is back, and in full effect. I inform him that Raisha and I will meet him at the one by the house in the South Park Plaza. He asks why he can't just come and pick us up from where we are staying, and I let him know that I'm not ready for that just yet. He disapprovingly agrees, and we disconnect our call. I climb out of bed and prepare to start my day. I throw out jogging outfits for me and Raisha and head over to Tasha's house so she can watch her for me while I treat myself to a spa day.

I end up going to Head Quarter's Salon & Spa, not

far from Tasha's house. I got the full salon package, which included a rosemary mint body wrap, a full-body relaxation massage, a botanical resurfacing facial, an aromatherapy scalp massage, a mani/pedi, and even a light lunch, all for only $400. When I walked out of those doors, boy was I rejuvenated! I called Tasha as I jumped in my car and told her I was on my way to get my hair set. When I finally get back, Raisha and Tasha are on the couch watching SpongeBob. I have to really give it to Tasha—her home is beautiful.

She stays in a three-bedroom, two-and-a-half-bath condo, and if I say so myself, the bitch is bad! She has this thing for zebra print, so most of her house is decorated in that theme. Her living room consists of a white Milano Ice Sectional, with black, white, and brown zebra-print throw pillows, and a matching zebra-print ottoman. On top of her cherry wood floor is a throw rug, the exact same color brown as in her pillows. Her coffee and end tables sit high and are chocolate brown. The living room is complete with a chocolate-brown entertainment center, with a 50" Plasma on top of it. I am so proud of her 'cause she's doing the damn thing—I guess being a real estate agent is really paying off.

"How was the spa?" Tasha asks, folding her legs underneath her body.

"Girl, it was wonderful. I have never felt so relaxed in my whole entire life!" I exclaim. "We gotta go there together one of these days," I tell her as I pick Raisha up and take her seat on the couch, placing her on my lap.

"Hell yeah! I sure need to relax, 'cause them damn home buyers be working my nerves! They kill me wanting to be picky as hell, when they barely got credit, not much money down, wanting to get an attitude with me like it's my fault!" she tells me, laughing.

"What they be doing, Tash?" I ask, pumping her up, knowing she's gonna get all animated with the story.

"Okay, let's say they want a three-bedroom, two-bathroom house, and their budget is around 200 grand. They got a 7% interest rate, so their mortgage payments are gonna be around $1500 a month. These damn dummies know that they can only get up to a 200 grand house, but they want to look at houses in the 250 to 300 price range. They're talking about how they need houses way bigger then what I'm showing them. I'm like, what the hell! Yo' ass all ready stretching your money to the max as it is. Who the hell do y'all think I am, Houdini?" she says, throwing her hands up in the air. I am on the couch in tears laughing at her silly ass, because the look on her face is so serious. I can just picture how she be looking at her clients!

After bullshitting with Tasha for a little while longer and getting my hair set, Raisha and I bid her farewell. By the time we get to the room it's a little after six, so I put her in the bath with me, and prepare for the evening. It's pretty nice out, so I dress Raisha according to the weather. She has on some blue Baby Phat jeans with pink stripes going down each side of her legs. She's wearing a white Baby Phat shirt with a pink cat on the front, pink and white Air Maxx, and the matching blue jean jacket just in case it gets cool later. I clasp her diamond-studded "Daddy's Girl" chain on her neck and place her gold bangle on her wrist. My baby was dressed and ready.

I, on the other hand, choose the "grown and sexy" look; I wanted Raimone to see what he was missing out on for this past week. I opted to wear dark blue, skin-tight Baby Phat jeans, a white sweater vest with a pink sequined cat on the right side. I have on white Baby Phat opened-toed sandals, with the same sequins across the toe and around the ankle strap. I put on my pink diamond tear-drop necklace and earring set, tennis bracelet, and fill my white Baby Phat hobo up with my belongings. When I take the rollers out of my hair, soft curls frame my pretty face, giving me an angelic look. I grab my light pink soft leather jacket out of the hotel's closet and close the door.

It is 7:30 on the dot when we arrive at Red Lobster, and Raimone is already inside. He called me a couple of minutes prior to tell me that it was kinda crowded, and that he went inside to secure us a table. I walk up to the hostess and informed her that my party is already seated, and she leads the way. Raimone stands up to greet us, and I can tell he is impressed by what I had on, because he was damn-near drooling. Mission accomplished!

I'm not really one to talk, because he was looking good enough to eat. He had on Sean John jeans, with a tan, brown, and blue Sean John button up, and some fresh butter Tims. He had on his chain, earrings, and he looked like he got a fresh cut and line up. The killing part was the way he was licking them damn lips; he was cheating now, 'cause he knew that shit drove me crazy! Breathe Sasha, breathe girl!

"Hey, Daddy!" Raisha yells, tapping him on the leg, breaking the silence.

"Hey, Rai Rai, give your Daddy a kiss," he says, picking her up and placing kisses on her little cheeks. After placing her in the high chair, he takes a seat and looks me in the eyes.

"How have you been, Sash?" he asks.

"Fine," I say, being short. I haven't let those juicy lips throw me off track.

"I ain't ask you how you looked, I asked you how you been," he flirts, smiling and licking those damn lips again. He reaches across the table and moves a curl from in front of my eye, and I blush slightly.

"Hi, my name is Chrissy," interrupts our waitress. "Our specials for the day are the Endless Shrimp, and our fresh fish of the day is tilapia. What can I get you to drink this evening?" She was short and a bit heavyset, but she carried it well. I order Raisha a raspberry lemonade, myself a Bahama Mama, and Raimone a Corona. With that, she disappears. Raimone plays with Raisha until the waitress returns with our drinks and a basket of biscuits.

"Are you ready to order now," the waitress asks, "or do you need a little more time?"

"No, we know exactly what we want," I said. "As an appetizer, we'll have the lobster, crab, and seafood stuffed mushrooms. As the entrée, I'll have the Ultimate Feast, with the Caesar salad and baked potato with extra sour cream and butter. He'll have New York strip and Rock Lobster tail, well done, also with a Caesar salad and baked potato. She'll have the Chicken Tenders with barbeque sauce, French fries, and a side of apple sauce." I was hoping like hell she got everything. Miraculously the waitress repeated everything perfectly and walked off to put the order in.

"So baby, like I was saying, how have you and Raisha been?" Raimone asked again once she was out of earshot.

"We've been good, Raimone, how have you been?"

I asked, taking a sip of my fruity drink.

"Miserable. Without the two people who matter to me in life, I've been going through it," he tells me with so much sincerity, that I honestly believe him.

"Well if you wouldn't have been doing stupid shit, we'd be at home now, wouldn't we?" I tell him, not letting up.

"You're right, Sash, I can't blame anybody but myself. I fucked up! All I'm asking is that if you give me another chance. I promise you, you won't regret it," he claims, covering my small hands with his.

"All that sounds good," I argue back. "But how do I know for sure that this shit won't happen again? You're asking me to put my heart back on the line, for the unknown. How do I know that you won't meet another bitch that can make shit happen for you, and that you'd do the same thing? All I saying is, how can I be sure that this is real?" I tell him, as the tears in my eyes threaten to fall. I unfold the napkin, and gently dab them away.

"You can be sure, because this is your man here, baby. You know me—" he protests.

"No, I thought I knew you!" I blurt out, cutting him off. I look around the restaurant to make sure nobody has noticed my sudden outburst. Once I'm sure nobody is paying us any mind, I tone it down a notch before I continue. "The Raimone that I thought I knew wouldn't be causing me this pain right now. Raimone, all I've ever done was love you, and this is how you repay me? My only question to you is, was the money she brought you worth it?" I ask him, looking him directly in the eyes. I wanted to see to his soul.

"My honest answer is: no, Sash; and if I could do it again, I would've never hurt you. You and Raisha are my life. I can't breathe without y'all. This past week has been pure hell, and I can't see this continuing any longer. So baby please come on home, I'm begging you," he says, wiping my face with his thumb where my new tears have fallen.

"Here's your appetizer," Chrissy says, placing the stuffed mushrooms in the middle of the table. Once she notices that my face is covered in tears, she quickly says, "I'm sorry, I didn't mean to interrupt."

"That's fine Chrissy, thank you. I was headed to the bathroom anyway," I say as I excuse myself. Once inside the bathroom, I look in the mirror and notice that my eyes are red and puffy. I pull my hair behind both of my ears so that it won't get wet and I splash a couple of handfuls of water on my face. I then proceed to dry it off with some paper towels. After composing myself, I head back to the table. Back at the table I notice that the food has arrived, and Raisha is smiling at me with a ketchup-dipped French fry in her hand.

"Hey, Mommy!" she chirps.

"Hey, Baby," I say back, placing a kiss on her little forehead. I slide into the booth, pick up a stuffed mushroom, and pop it in my mouth. I close my eyes to savor the taste. Oh how I love these things! Raimone cuts off a piece of his steak and holds it out for me to taste. It melts in my mouth, right along with those cheddar biscuits that I like so much. We eat the rest of the meal in silence, until Chrissy comes by and places a sundae in front of Raisha.

"Oh, Chrissy. we didn't order a sundae," I inform her.

"Don't worry about it, it's on me. Can you I get you guys any dessert?" she asks. I guess she's still feeling bad about catching me crying.

"Baby do you want anything?" Raimone asks. After I shake my head no, he asks her to bring the check. In a couple of minutes, she's placing the check on the table, face down.

"Thank you, Chrissy. Here, I can take care of this right now," Raimone says, catching her before she gets too far away. He peels off a hundred dollar bill and hands it to her.

"Ok sir, I'll be back with your change. Can I get you guys any boxes?" she asks

"No, we are fine, and keep the change." I tell her with a warm smile.

"Thank you and you guys enjoy the rest of your evening," she says graciously, happy of the fact that she just received a twenty dollar tip. I clean Raisha up with a Wet Wipe, put on both of our jackets, and hand her to Raimone. Once outside he walks us to my car and fastens her into her car seat. He then comes around to my side just as I pulling my seat belt across my lap. I start the car and roll down my window.

"So you never answered my question," he drawls, leaning into the window.

"I'll call you later, Raimone," I tell him. With a look of disappointment, he nods his head "yeah," kisses me on the forehead, and walks away.

Chapter Eleven

Raimone

I'm telling you, man, Sasha fucked me up by not coming home with me tonight. I thought for sure that we were gonna be making love at this very moment. I am hoping and praying that I didn't fuck this up for us. It broke my heart to see those tears falling from her eyes tonight, and it felt even worse to know that I'm the one to cause them. I know you're probably thinking, if I cared so much, why did I do the shit that I did, right? Well let me answer that question for you: I don't have a clue! I do know for a fact that if I would've told her the truth, that she would never come back to me. I mean how can you tell your wife (whom you've been with for almost nine years) that you have another child? That's not even the really bad part, how do you tell her that the other child is a year older than your supposedly only child? This is some real Jerry Springer shit for real and I'm caught all up in the middle of it.

My cell vibrates, and when I glance at the screen I see that Taisha has sent me yet another text message. It reads:

"Mone I dn't kno wut ur prob is, but u need 2 call me. I can't function w/o u n my life, me & Moni need u. Please call."

Ok, I feel bad for hurting her, but I just can't do it. I can't lose my family fucking with her. She broke the rules, man! If she would have never called Sasha that night, we'd be cool; but she fucked it up, not me.

I go home and sit on the couch watching ESPN to catch some sports highlights. I end up dozing off for a few hours. I wake up around 2 a.m. and realize that Sasha has yet to call. I flip open my cell, and give her a call instead.

"Hello."

"Hey, Bay, what you doing?" I ask.

She says, "Nothing much, sitting here watching 'Martin You So Crazy' on HBO. What you doing?"

"Thinking about you and Raisha. Why didn't you call me?" I ask, wondering why she's up this late and hasn't once called me.

"I was gonna call you in the morning, Raimone; is there something that you need?" she questions, sounding like she's ready to get off the phone.

"Well, actually no, I just wanted to see what you guys were doing. If you're busy, I can let you go," I say, knowing that she's gonna tell me that she isn't busy.

"Yeah I am, so I'll call you tomorrow, okay?" she says, busting my fucking bubble.

"That's fine," I say, adding, "I love you." I never got a reply, because by then she had already hung up. What the fuck have I done? Please don't let my baby leave me.

Chapter Twelve

Sasha

"Hell, yeah, girl, he sounded like a lost puppy on the phone!" I laugh as I tell Tasha about the conversation wih Raimone. "I didn't even tell him back that I loved him; I just hung up! I bet he's been calling this phone all damn day; too bad I cut it off."

"Girl, he gone kick yo' ass when he see you! Why you playing with the man like that? You know you're going home," Tasha says, giggling.

"I know that, and you know that, but he doesn't know that," I explain. "I got one more day here, and I ain't wasting my damn money, fuck that! I'll go home tomorrow when I check out. I told you I'm gonna show his ass better than I can tell him. He'll know not to fuck with Sasha again!" I say, still laughing. I've been avoiding Raimone for a whole day, and the shit is funny as hell to me. That's how I felt when I was waiting up on his ass to come home that night; so, oh fucking well!

Because tomorrow's Friday, and I will be headed back to work on Monday, I decided to take Raisha out for a day of fun. I decided to take her to the Memphis Kiddie Park, in Cleveland. It's a nice place for kids to have fun. The place is equipped with little roller coasters, water boats, mini golf, a train, and even a small Ferris wheel. We went there last year with Raimone, but that was a long time ago, so I know she'll enjoy it. It's 2 o'clock, so I get us ready before it gets too crowded. I place several pony tails and barrettes in Raisha's hair, and we head to the park.

Boy, did she enjoy herself! She ate cotton candy and had a blast. I took so many pictures of her, it doesn't make any sense. I stop at McDonalds on the way back to the hotel, and she's in the back in her car seat, knocked out. I reach into my purse to retrieve my ringing phone, and what do you know? It's Raimone.

"Hello," I answer dryly.

"Damn, Sash, it's like that?" he asks, irritated.

"Like what, Raimone?" I ask, knowing damn well what he's talking about.

"Come on Sash, don't play dumb with me. I've been calling you for the past two days. You don't answer, you don't call, you can't say shit!" he yells over the phone.

"Hold the fuck up! It doesn't feel good when the shoe is on the other mu'fuckin foot does it?" I retort. "How the fuck do you think I felt when I was calling your phone all night, and you didn't answer 'cause you were laid up with yo' bitch! Tell me that, Raimone!" He pissed me off. Who the fuck did he think he was, calling my phone on some ole jealous shit. He got a lot of fucking nerve, if you ask me.

"Look Sash, I didn't call to argue with you," he says, sounding defeated.

"I know you didn't; and ain't bout to argue with you either, Raimone!" I yell; and with that, I hang up. Of course he called right back, only to be ignored. A couple of minutes later, my alert sounded letting me know that I had a new text message. It read:

"Look Bay I'm sorry I called on sum B.S but I'm ova here stressin w/o u. I luv u & I jus wanna b a fam again. Can u call me when u get a chance?"

"That's more fuckin' like it," I say as I toss the phone back into my Dooney and Burke tote. After washing Raisha up and tucking her into bed, I decide to give Raimone a call. The phone rang all of two times, and he answers out of breath.

"Hello," he says, breathing hard.

"You busy?" I ask.

"Hell, naw, Bay, I just had to get to the phone. I left it in the living room by mistake," he says. By now I have a smirk on my face, he this hard-ass thug nigga running to the phone like a schoolgirl.

"Oh, well, what are you doing?" I ask, beating around the bush.

"Nothing, just sitting here waiting on you to call to tell me that you're coming home. Sasha, I can't breathe without you here, girl; don't you know that? I know I fucked up, but I don't know what more I can say to make you see that I'm sorry. You've been gone for two weeks, and I don't think I can take another day."

"You being sorry isn't the problem. The problem is you doing me wrong." I tell him. "I gave you my heart, and in return you gave me your ass to kiss! I know you love me, Raimone, and you're a wonderful father to Raisha. The thing is, I've always told myself that I would never be a fool for a nigga, and that's what you're making me out to be. So I'm going to tell you like this: Fool me once, shame on you. Fool me twice, shame on me. If you fool me a second time, there isn't a third chance for you, or us. Do you understand what I'm saying to you?" I ask him, as tears stream down my face. I hate it when I get all emotional.

"Yes, I do, Sash, and this won't ever happen again," he promises me.

I'm not sure, but it sounds like he's crying on the other end of the phone.

"Well in that case, Raisha and I will be home tomorrow," I tell him.

"Thank you GOD! Do you need help with any of your things, 'cause I can come and get them for you," he says excitedly.

"No, I can handle everything just fine. Let me hang up now, and I'll see you when we get there in the morning. You will be home, won't you?" I asked, knowing damn well he better be.

"I wouldn't be anywhere else," he says, and we both end the call. I rest on the couch and feel good knowing that I'm going back home tomorrow. I can't wait to soak in my spa tub and sleep in my own bed. I know for sure that Raisha's gonna be happy to see her dad, even though she's too young to say anything, I know she misses him. I'm not going to lie, I miss is black ass too! With that as a last thought, I click off the nightlight beside the bed and drift off to sleep.

I awaken to a little hand rocking me gently back

and forth. When my eyes focus, I see my baby standing in front of me with a big smile on her face. I instantly snatch her in bed with me and attack her with tickles. She's laughing so hard, that it's making me laugh.

"Eat, eat, Mommy," she says to me after the tickling has stopped

"You hungry, Rai Rai?" I ask.

"Me eat, eat, Mommy," she says again, rubbing her little tummy.

With that I rise up out of the bed and proceed to start our day of moving back home. I make Raisha some pancakes and a couple of pieces of bacon. I wasn't hungry, so while she was eating, I begin packing our things back inside of our luggage. At 10:50 a.m., almost checkout time, I lug our suitcases down to my car. After doing that, I go into the lobby and check out, signing my copies and giving them back the key.

Once I strap Raisha securely in her car seat, we head home. I knew Raison was sitting on pins and needles, waiting on our return. I just hope I was doing the right thing. Something about this situation didn't sit right with me, but I shook it off as just being nervous. All I'm going to say is: Raimone better hope he's on the up and up; but for now, I am taking my ass home.

Chapter Thirteen

Sasha

We've been home for almost two weeks, and life couldn't be any better. I'm back at work, and Raimone is being the best man ever. Our anniversary was, coincidentally, last weekend and I can honestly say he surprised me with everything he had planned. I was on my way home from work last Friday when my mom calls, telling me that she is keeping Raisha for the weekend. I didn't think anything of it because my mom always likes having Raisha around. I headed home to change my clothes so that I could do a little shopping. When I pulled up to the driveway, I saw Raimone putting suitcases inside the trunk of his car. When he saw me he had a look of guilt on his face.

"What are you doing?" I asked, with my hand on

my hips, after getting out of my car and walking over to where he was standing.

He walked over to the passenger side of the car and opened it. "Just get in the car, Sasha."

"Where are we going?" I continued with the questions.

"Just get in the car Sash, please," he pleaded, and I walked over to my car to grab my purse. Slinging it over my shoulder, I climbed into the passenger seat of his car. I started to protest when he placed a blindfold over my eyes, but the look on his face allowed me to chill out. After closing the door, he got in the driver seat, started the car, but never said a word.

I sat in the car, wondering where the hell he's taking me, all the while blindfolded. We rode so long I started to doze off. Maybe an hour later I woke up when I felt the car stop. I heard Raimone get out of the car and open the trunk. A couple of seconds later, the passenger door opened and he reached for my hand, helping me out of the car. I walked a short distance and up a few steps before I heard a door open; we stepped inside. My mind was racing a-mile-a-minute about what the hell was going on, until he removed the blindfold.

"Raimone!" I exclaimed. It was beautiful! We were standing in the living room of a cabin. The living room had vaulted ceilings and a hunter green couch. An electric fireplace sat right in front of the couch. To the left was a full-size kitchen with stainless steel appliances and a wooden table and chairs. The cabinets were the same dark wood color as the walls, and there were ceiling fans throughout. There were French doors from the living room that lead to a covered hot tub, gas grill, and patio set. We walked toward the back of the cabin and the bedroom took the cake! There was a huge wooden king-size that had a heart made with rose petals on the black silk comforter. In the corner was a massage table, and to the side of it there were all types of oils. On the wooden nightstand was a bucket filled with ice, into which Raimone placed a bottle of wine. I turned around to thank him and there he was, standing there with a smile and a platter of chocolate-covered strawberries in his hand.

"Happy anniversary, Baby," he told me, kissing me on the lips.

I fell in love with him all over again that weekend. He gave me a full-body massage and fed me strawberries in the hot tub. We talked about the future. He told me how much he loved me and we spent the rest of the night making love. The next day was pretty much the same, and by Sunday I was once again happy to be Mrs. Raimone Ford. Since then he's been home taking care of me and Raisha, and I honestly can't complain. I really think he's learned his lesson; he hasn't been clubbing or anything. The only time he leaves the house is to make a drop to one of his runners or to go to the grocery store for something minor like bread or milk. The only reason that he's going out tonight is because it's Rob's birthday, and Rob is having a party at The Envy Lounge off of West 25th Street.

Shit, even with that being his boy, I had to make him go. I know you're probably thinking, what kind of bitch would make her husband go out to the club full of hoes? Raimone is a grown-ass man, and he's gonna do what he wants to do anyways. I figured that it doesn't make sense to force him stay in the house all of the time. That's what's wrong with women today, thinking that they can keep a man from cheating by staying up under him. That shit doesn't mean a damn thing, 'cause trust me, once he's out and about, he's gonna act a damn fool! Let your man run free. Listen to me when I tell you, if he wants to cheat, then that's what he's gonna do, no matter what. So I say: Go out and have fun, enjoy yourself!

It's almost 11:30 when Raimone steps into the living room, ready to go. I look him up and down, and he really looks good. He has on dark blue Rocawear jeans, a white and tan Rocawear track jacket, with the tan symbol on the upper side of his chest, tan stripes down the zipper, the waist, and the wrist. He has on a plain white t-shirt, a tan Rocawear belt that had a huge gold "R" on it, and new butter Tim's. Include his chain, Movado watch, blinging-ass diamond studs, and the fact that he's smelling like my favorite cologne (Jean Paul Gaultier), my baby was the shit!

"You look nice," I tell him, smiling appreciatively.

"Thanks. You sure you want me to go, 'cause I could stay her with you if you like," he says, taking a seat next to me on the couch.

"Go ahead, Baby. Enjoy yourself tonight. It's your best friend's birthday. I'm not going to do anything tonight but take a shower and go to bed, I'm really tired. There isn't much more to do, because Raisha's already sleeping," I tell him as I stand up, place my small hands inside his, and pull him into a standing position. "Now get out of here," I order, pushing him toward the door. After he opens the door, he turns to me and plants the sweetest kiss on my lips.

"What was that for?" I ask.

"Just for being you, Sash, I love you," he says.

"I love you, too, Raimone; have fun," I say as I close

and lock the front door. I turn off the TV in the living room and head to my room where I run my shower.

Sitting on bed after my shower, I apply lotion evenly on my entire body. Because vanilla is my favorite scent, I opted to use my Vanilla Lace body cream by Victoria Secret. Once I'm done, I prop myself up on one of the many pillows on my bed and just look around. To me, my bedroom was the best place in the house. I had a huge wood California King poster bed that swallowed my little ass whole once I laid down on it. Actually the whole seven-piece bedroom set was huge, from the armoire down to the nightstand. When I saw it at the store I had to have it. I knew I couldn't just hand the sales associate the $11,000 that it cost after taxes, so I charged it to my American Express.

That's another thing that separates me from these other women out here: I have A1 credit, and I use it to my advantage every chance I get. Raimone always taught me to never spend large amounts of cash in any store, because once it's over the $10,000 limit, the store has to be report the purchase to the IRS.

He was shocked at first when I told him how much the bedroom set cost that I had just purchased, but that shock wore off fast when it was delivered. You couldn't take the smile off his face when I told him that it was called California King. To this day he still says that our bed isn't for everybody; I'm guessing he thinks he's a king or some shit.

My train of thought breaks at the sound of my baby calling my name. I climb out of my bed, and head into her room.

"Mommy," Raisha cries out.

"Here I am, Baby," I say as I bend down to pick her

up. I carry her back into my room and put her down gently on my bed. She is back sleeping in a matter of minutes, just like I knew she would. I guess she just wanted to be close to me, and I didn't mind it one bit. As I looked at my sleeping daughter's face, I couldn't help but smile. Raimone and I sure did a good job when we created Raisha. I closed my eyes, and I thought back to the first day I met him.

I was fifteen and it was the last day of school; Tasha and I were across the street from Max Hayes, waiting on the bus. The 326 was always packed, so we knew there was no way that most of the students standing there were going to fit on the already-crowded bus. So we decided to walk down to W. 25th St. and catch the Circulator to our house. We were one street over when this Burgundy Regal with tinted windows slows down beside us, and the driver door opens. Tasha and I exchanged glances as to let one another know that we were going to kick who-ever's ass together if they started some shit.

My heart was beating a-mile-a-minute, because I'm ready for whatever. That was until I see the cutest boy I've ever seen step out of the car and casually walk over to us.

"How can we help you?" Tasha said, leaning to one side, hands on her hips, ready for action.

"I come in peace, Lil Mama," he says as he holds his hands up in mock surrender. "My name is Mone, and I'm trying to holla at Shorty right here," he says pointing to me. He didn't know it, but I was melting inside.

"Well, Mone, what is your government? Cause mine ain't Lil Mama, and hers damn sho ain't Shorty," Tasha advises him, putting an emphasis on the names that he'd given us. I just stand there all the while, taking it all in. I was giggling on the inside because I know he's standing there thinking, "No, this lil-ass girl ain't poppin fly like she grown!" Instead he uncrosses his arms from across his chest and strokes his small goatee like he was in deep thought.

"Okay, how about this?" he said as he dropped his arms and rubs his hands together. "Hello, my name is Raimone, and I was coming over to see if I can have a few words with this beautiful young lady here." He points to me once again.

"A lot better," Tasha says and walks away. She turns and looks over her shoulder at me, and mouthed, "He's cute." I laugh because Tasha is a damn trip, but I love her crazy ass. "I'll be at the bus stop. Holla if you need me. You know I got my shit in the bag, and I ain't afraid to use it," she says, laughing.

"A feisty one, isn't she?" he observed.

I smile, "Yeah, she is, but I love her."

"So can I have the privilege of knowing your name, Pretty Girl?" he asked politely.

"Sasha. My name is Sasha, and that's my twin, Tasha," I said, pointing and blushing at the same time.

"Well, Sasha, how old are you? And do you have a boyfriend?" he asked.

"I'm 15, and no I don't." I drop my eyes and look at him from his shoes up. He's wearing black and red Air Jordans, blue jean Levi shorts, a black T-shirt with a red Jordan symbol on the front, and a matching hat. Every time he cocked his head to the side, his earring sparkled under the sun. I was feeling his style and I believe he knew it.

"Ok, well, that's good, at least I ain't gotta take you

from nobody," he smiled.

Listen to me when I tell you, his teeth were gorgeous.

"Can I get your number, so that I can call you sometime?" he inquired.

"Yeah, do you have a pen?" Apparently he didn't, because he jogs back to the car and returns with a pen and paper. As I'm jotting down my number, I heard Tasha telling me that the Circulator is coming. I pushed my information into his hand and ran to catch up with her at the bus stop. As soon as I bend the corner, the bus is pulling up.

"I would've taken you home," I heard. It was Raimone, idling beside the bus, in the driver seat of the car I assumed was his. The bus door opened, and Tasha and I stepped on.

"Sorry Boo, I don't know you like that." I told with a smile, while the bus doors are closing. The bus pulls off headed toward our destination.

We lived in a nice four-bedroom house on West 11th, not far from our school, with our parents Monique and Phillip Jones. Our mother (everyone called her Nikki) worked as an RN at Grace Hospital around the corner from our house. While our father (everyone called him Phil) worked downtown as a manager at a construction company called Formation. They both made pretty good money, so it was no problem to give us everything wanted and more. We were the only two children, so being spoiled was an understatement. We had our own room, with separate phone lines, and all of the flyest gear. To most people we had it all, and honestly we did. In fact the only reason that we didn't have a car was because we weren't old enough to drive yet. Daddy told us that as soon as we turned fifteen and a half, he was signing us up for driving school, and we only had three months to go. Tash and I were best friends, so we didn't mind sharing a car. Hell, we went everywhere together anyways.

After taking off our shoes at the door, we both plopped down on the couch. Mommy didn't play about her white carpet, and she'd kick our ass for sitting on her couch that way if she were home—but she wasn't home, now was she? I turned on the TV and instantly I was bobbing my head to Foxy Brown's new video from the How to Be a Player soundtrack. My groove was interrupted by the ringing phone in my bedroom; I jumped up rushing to it, stubbing my toe on the end table in the process.

"Shit!" I yelled as I made it to the phone just as the ringing stopped. I checked the caller ID but no luck there, because it merely said "unknown caller." I bent down to tend to my toe to stop the intense pain. Pissed that I hurt my damn toe and still missed the call, I headed back toward the living room. As I took a seat back on the couch, I looked over at Tasha only to see her holding her stomach, laughing hard as hell.

"What's so fucking funny?" I asked.

"Yo ole' thirsty ass about to kill ya damn self running for the phone! You didn't even check and make sure your foot was alright until after you missed the call," she says as tears fall from her eyes. The sight is so funny, that I couldn't do nothing but join in.

Rubbing my toe again, I said, "Fuck you! It wasn't my foot, it was my toe, and this bitch really hurt." This only makes her laugh harder, so I throw one of the pillows off the couch at her. She catches it, prepared to toss it back, when my phone rings again. This time

I take my damn time, because I might lose my toe this time and I wasn't having that. It's the "unknown caller" again, so I snatch it up with an attitude, thinking that maybe it's a wrong number.

I barked into the receiver: "Hello!"

"Hello, can I speak to Sasha?" the person asked, and instantly I know that it's Raimone.

Playing around, I teased, "This is her, may I ask who's calling?"

"It's Raimone," he countered.

"Raimone who?" I said.

"Oh it's like that, huh?" he observed, laughing.

We stayed on the phone for hours, talking about everything under the sun. I found out that he was about to be 17, and that he'd be a senior next year at South High School. He was an only child, and he lived on 53rd in Fleet with his grandmother, Delores. I told him all about me and my family, and if I say so myself, the conversation went pretty well. This went on for about two weeks straight, him calling me and us staying on the phone until one of us would fall asleep. The funniest was when he went to sleep first and lied about it. I heard him breathing hard on my end, so I knew he was asleep. After calling his name a couple of times, I'd hung up. He'd called right back telling me he was awake; that went on all night until he really passed out.

Eventually he started coming over to sit on the porch, until it was time for me to head into the house. Raimone was a good guy; he was respectful and seemed to have his head on straight. My mother and father thought that he was a complete gentleman. That's why they had no problem with me going to the movies with him one Friday night. We ended up going to Tower City to see

Face Off, starring John Travolta and Nicolas Cage. We got there early and because we had an hour to spare before our movie was to start, we decided to have a couple slices of pizza and Pepsi at Sbarro's. Once it was time for the movie, he bought popcorn and we took our seats. It had an exciting plot and we were happy to be together.

"I loved that movie!" I squealed as we went down the escalator to the parking garage.

Opening the passenger door for me, he said, "Yeah, it was pretty good." I slid inside. We talked a little bit more about the movie as he drove, and before we knew it, we were in front of my house. He killed the engine and we sat quietly, until I broke the silence.

"I really had a nice time tonight, Raimone," I said.

"I did too," he told me, "but this is only the beginning."

Confused, I asked, "The beginning of what?"

He looked at me with a serious face. "The beginning of our life together. You're going to be my wife one day, Sasha, even if you don't know it yet."

I blushed, "Is that right!"

"Yup," he nodded. He continued to tell me that that it was the beginning of many dates, and he didn't lie. It was official: I was Raimone Ford's girlfriend, and I was proud of it. I was his date at his prom, and he was my date at my prom. Years later we're married, have a beautiful daughter and a happy home.

I come out of my stroll down memory lane when Raisha shifts slightly in her sleep. I kiss her softly on the cheek, cut out the light on the night stand, and drift off to sleep.

Chapter Fourteen

Naitaisha

I'm sitting here tripping the fuck out. It's been a whole fucking month and that bitch Raimone has yet to call! Shit, he hasn't answered any of my calls, voicemails, or texts. What type of shit is this? I do not understand how the hell he can just write me and my daughter out of his life like we are disposable. I bet he's over there catering to that bitch's every fucking need, while I'm over here losing my damn mind. I really can't see what has his ass so sprung off this bitch, I mean honestly I can't. The bitch ain't got shit on me. If you ask me she's ugly—flat out!

Maybe he can't leave her because of all the money he has invested in her ass. Even then, that doesn't' make right what he's doing to me and my baby. I've been so distraught by this shit, that I haven't seen my own child in almost a month. I can't bear to look in her face, because when I do I just see her daddy. I know it's fucked up, but if I can't have Raimone, I don't want any part of him. I love my daughter—don't get me wrong. It's just that I can't take care of her by myself. So my mom agreed to take her in until I get myself together, which hopefully will be soon. Her birthday is less than three weeks away, and I have plans that everything's going back to normal by then. All I have to do is get a chance to talk to Raimone; once he hears what I have to say, he'll be back.

Ringggggggggggggg, ringggggggggggg. I stretch my arm to grab the phone, all the while hoping like hell it's Raimone.

"Hello," I say tentatively.

"What's up, Bitch?" Big Pat's loud-ass mouth yells through the receiver.

"Nothing," I say, dry as hell.

"What you getting into tonight?" she asks.

"Shit, watching a lil bit of TV," I state as I twirl a small piece of my hair around my finger.

"I was asking," she says, "because Tiff and I are heading to The Envy tonight and wanted to see if you would like to come."

"I don't know, Pat, I'm not really feeling up to it tonight," I say.

"Damn, Taisha, we ain't kicked it in a nice-ass minute! We yo' mutha'fuckin girls, and you been brushing us off like we did something to you. If we did, please let it be known, cause I kinda miss yo ole' yellow ass!" she tells me, laughing.

"What time should I be ready?" I ask, giving in.

"I'll be there at eleven," she says and hangs up in my ear. I look at the receiver in disbelief, because that bitch is a damn trip. I glance at the clock and realize that I have more than enough time to get me an outfit, so I head to Parma Town mall.

Once inside the mall I walk to Demo, my favorite store of all time. I shop around for a minute and take a couple of items into the dressing room. Once I'm satisfied with my choice, I pay at the register and head on home. I bathe, flat iron my hair, and apply a little bit of makeup. I have a little less than an hour to dress. I lay everything that I may need on my bed, just so I don't forget anything.

Once I'm fully dressed, I stand in front of my full-length mirror, looking at perfection. The outfit is the perfect fit, and I am happy with my decision. I have on black jean capris with Ecko Red written in silver down the left leg. They were cuffed at the bottom and stitched in silver. My shirt was also black, with a silver, glitter-like dinosaur on the left lower half of my stomach. Across my breast it said Ecko Red, also in silver. I had on silver strappy sandals, silver bangles, earrings, and silver necklace. I fill my silver clutch with the necessities and wait for Pat to arrive. I wait all of five minutes before I hear her ghetto ass blowing like a crazed maniac outside my house. I cut off the lights, grab my keys, and head out the door. I hop into her Ford Explorer and we are on our way.

I'm actually enjoying myself, and I happy that I agreed to come. Shit, I needed to get out. My night was about to get even better, and I didn't even know it. We are sitting at the bar, and I am on my third Henney and Coke when I hear, "Taisha, ain't that yo baby daddy ova there?" It was Tiff asking me that as she pointed over toward the door. My head jerks around instantly toward direction that she was pointing. Low and behold it was Raimone, in the mutha'fuckin flesh. I climb off of the bar stool and head straight for his ass. He had his back toward me, giving some dude dap, so he didn't see me quickly approaching.

"You can't call me back, but yo' ass out at the bar partying, huh?" I ask, leaning into his ear. He turns around slowly and looks me directly in the face. To be sure, that shocked look on his face meant that he wasn't expecting to see me.

"Taisha, don't start no shit in here, girl," Ramoine says hopefully, calmly, looking around the bar.

"Oh, you ain't gotta worry about that, Boo. I was just saying, what's up," I say as I turn and switch away. You see that was a part of my plan. I couldn't let the nigga know that he had me still sprung. I walked back over to the table, smiling like a cat that just swallowed a canary.

"Why you all smiley, Bitch?" Tiff asks as soon as my ass hit the bar stool.

"Damn, Bitch, you all nosey and shit!" I laugh. "Naw for real, I'm smiling cause that nigga can't get enough of me. I'm leaving with him tonight, so when it's time to go, y'all ain't gotta wait."

Now I know damn well I'm lying, but they don't know that. How can I tell my girls that this nigga dogged the fuck out of me and stopped answering my phone calls? You're right, I can't. And I ain't about to try to either. Fuck that. I tell them that I'm headed to the bar, but instead I slide out the door to see where Raimone is parked, to put my plan in motion. It was last call when

Tiff and Pat get up to head out, which couldn't have been perfect timing.

"You call me when you get home, Taisha," Pat says. I assure her that I will, tell Tiff 'bye, and they are on their way. About ten minutes later I notice that Raimone is giving some of his boys dap and is about to head out, so I quickly make my move. I slide past him undetected and run out to where his car is parked.

He walks up with a confused look on his face, looking at me like I am crazy for leaning against his car. "Taisha, what the fuck you doing?" My head is inside of my hands, so I slowly lift the face up and look at him with tear-filled eyes.

"I need a ride, Mone," I say, casting him a pitiful look. I go on to tell him that me and Pat got into it and that they left me at the bar with no ride. He looks around for a minute, I guess trying to see if my story adds up, then unlocks the door so that I can get in. We ride in silence for a couple of minutes until I take my act a little further. I pull my keys out of my purse, set them on my lap, and start gagging.

"Taisha, don't throw up in my damn car," he warns and pulls over to the side of the road.

"I'm not, Mone, it's just that I'm sick, and my head is spinning like crazy," I say, putting on an Oscar-winning performance. We drive off and I lay my head back against the seat, closing my eyes. About ten minutes later, I feel the car stop. I figure that we're in front of my house, so I continue to fake sleep.

"Taisha, we're here, get up," Raimone says, slightly nudging me, trying to wake me up from my fake-ass sleep. "Taisha," he calls again, but I continue to lay there. I finally exhale when I hear him kill the engine and open the driver-side door. Moments later the passenger door opens, he grabs my keys out of my lap, and carries me up the stairs to my house. Once the door is open, he carries me upstairs to my bedroom and lays me gently on what used to be our bed. I hear him preparing to leave, and I sit up slowly, acting like I'm still out of it.

"Thank you, Raimone," I say softly.

"No problem, Tai," he replies and continues his stride down the hall.

"Can you do me a favor?" I ask, before he could hit the stairs. "Can you hand me two Tylenol and a bottled water out of the fridge over there?" I say, pointing to the small refrigerator that I had inside of my bedroom. While he's inside the bathroom, I quickly remove my pants, kick them to the floor, and slide under the covers. He brings me everything I asked for. I swallow the small pills in one big gulp.

"Are you going to be alright, Tai?" he asks, and I can see in his eyes that he actually cares.

"I would be better if you stay with me for a while," I say. He takes off his jacket, lays it on my chair, and sits on the edge of my bed. I curl up close to him and savor the feeling of being close to him again. He slowly runs his hands through my hair, and it feels so good that I start to softly moan. "What happened to us, Mone?" I ask him, on the verge of crying.

"Come on, Tai, don't start this," he says sternly.

"It's only a question. I'm a big girl, I can handle it," I announce as I push my hair behind my ears and sit up straight to stare him in the eyes.

"Tai, you over stepped your boundaries when you called my house," he plainly states.

"I know, Raimone," I cry, "and I've said I was sorry

over and over again. How long are you gonna hold that against me? I love you, and this is hurting me."

Overwhelmed with emotion, I kiss him hard and deep on the mouth. When he doesn't resist, I straddle him and rub my fingers softly through his hair. I break the kiss, push him back up against the headboard, and slowly unzip his pants. His chocolate stick springs to life out of his boxers, and I try my best to swallow that mutha'fucka whole. I know it's feeling damn good to him, because his eyes are closed and he's groaning from deep in his soul. I suck his dick like my life is depending on it, and to me it does. I know it's not gonna take him long to cum, because with the skills I got, it never does. I use my free hand to take my panties off, and kick them away.

"Damn, Tai, what you doing to me, girl? Ahhhh, shit!" he shouts out, on the verge of cumming. I take my mouth off his dick and quickly replace with it my pussy. At first I bounce on him slowly, but then I speed up because it feels so damn good. Next thing I know, I'm on my back and Raimone is digging deep into my guts. He is fucking me so hard that it should've hurt, but instead it felt so damn good.

"Fuck this pussy, boy," I moan into his ear while he's pounding away at my insides. I think he's trying to teach me a lesson by how hard he's ramming it in, but my freaky-ass doesn't mind.

He places his hands around my neck and he begins to choke me. This may sound weird to you, but it seems like it makes the sex even better. The harder he chokes me, the better I feel! He must've been trying to prove a point because he was fucking and choking the shit out of me! I guess he notices that my face was turning red from the lack of oxygen, because he loosens his grip but continues to punish my pussy.

"Don't stop, baby, right there…right there! Shit, don't stop, this feels so fucking good!" I cry out in ecstasy as I throw my hips back at him, and we cum in unison. Minutes later we're lying in my bed panting and trying to catch our breaths. I slowly crawl over to him and place my head on his chest. I know that he isn't going to stay the night, so there was no time like the present to tell him my good news. "Raimone, I've got something to tell you," I say as I make circles on his chest with my finger.

"What's that?" he asks, sounding exhausted.

"I'm pregnant," I tell him.

He sits up so fast that I nearly fall off the edge of the bed.

"What!" he yells, standing up.

"I said I'm pregnant, fourteen weeks to be exact." I smile.

"Are you fucking serious?" he asks as he put his boxers and pants on in a hurry. "This shit can't be fuckin' happening! Wait a minute, ain't you supposed to be on the pill?"

"Yes I was on the pill." I lie. "But everybody knows that they aren't a hundred percent effective." In fact, the pill was zero percent effective for me, because I stopped taking the pills a long time ago. "What's the problem?" I ask frantically, because I'm confused.

"What's the problem?" he stares at me, incredulous. "The problem, Taisha, is the fact that I'm married, and I shouldn't be having any outside kids on my wife. The problem is," he continues, "that I don't even fuck with you like that anymore. The problem is," he was screaming now, "that I'm trying to make it work with my wife, and every time I turn around it's another one of my fuck-ups added to the list!"

"Fuck-up?" I retort. "Are you saying that me being pregnant, and our daughter, are your fuck-ups?" I yell, getting in his face. I'm not giving a damn that I'm naked as hell from the waist down, and his cum is dripping down my leg.

"Yeah," he answers, "that's what I'm saying, Taisha. This whole situation is fucked up! I have a loving wife at home who would do anything that I ask her. I'm not satisfied with that, because I'm over here getting my dick sucked by a bitch who I don't give a shit about!" he roars. Raimone has a cold look in his eyes, so I instantly know that he's serious.

"Is that how you feel about me, Raimone?" I sob, clutching my chest and falling to my knees. My heart is in pieces and there was nothing that I could do about it. Raimone reaches into his pocket and pulls out a knot of money. He counts out around a thousand dollars and sits the cash on my night stand.

"Get rid of it," he says as he walks out, meaning the baby, leaving me broken on the floor.

I want to tell him that I had an ultrasound and even though they aren't sure, it could be the boy that he has always wanted. But he was long gone. I lay on the floor in that same spot, crying my eyes out, until the wee hours of the morning. It seemed so unreal to me. How could he treat me like this after he told me that he loved me? I swear I went through all of the emotions, lying here all night.

I wonder if this is how my mom felt when my father "just so happened" to forget about us. I'm not going to end up like her. I'm not going to let a man break me down. I got something for his ass and it's not gonna be pretty! Trust me when I tell you, Raimone and his bitch will pay for my pain—just watch and see!

Chapter Fifteen

Raimone

The whole ride from Taisha's house I kept replaying the conversation over again in my mind, and my head is killing me. I can't believe I got myself into this fucked-up situation once again! I knew she wasn't lying, 'cause she was to fucking excited. If she honestly thought that I was gonna be happy about hearing that shit, she was crazy for real.

"What the fuck!" I yell as I bang my hands against my steering wheel. I hope she does the right thing and gets rid of it, but I know deep down that she isn't going to. She going to have that baby, and honestly I can't blame no one but myself. So now I'm going to have three kids, but my wife only knows about the one that we have. How in the hell am I going to be able to continue to hide this shit from Sasha?

I notice that it's a little bit after four by the time I pull up outside of my house. I slowly open the front door, and I'm instantly greeted with darkness. I reach out to the knob on the wall and adjust the lights so that I can see and continue through the house. I check on Raisha first and notice that she's not in her bed, so our bedroom is my next destination. Both of my girls are in the bed sleeping peacefully, and all I can do if feel like shit. I grab some boxers out of the drawer, take off my clothes, and head to the shower.

As I stand in the shower and wash Taisha's juices off of me, I can't help but feel bad for her. She's right when she says that all she does is love me, and that all of this is my fault. My thoughts shift to Sasha and what would happen if she were to find out everything that I've been trying so hard to hide. She'd leave me without a doubt, and I'm absolutely sure she'll take my Rai-Rai away and I can't have that. That's my baby, and Daddy's Princess can't go anywhere. I know what you're probably thinking: Why is it so easy for me to walk away from Moni? Moni is my daughter also, and I love her as well; but she wasn't planned. I didn't want Taisha to have her and I wasn't there when she was born. Shit, I barely even see her because she's always with Taisha's mom.

Taisha hardly ever has Moni, but she's always hoopin' and hollering about me not spending enough time with the child. Like I said before, Taisha is not girlfriend material. All she wants to do is shop, club, drink, and fuck. She doesn't have any long-term goals. Shit, she doesn't even have a damn job! Taisha is going to be Taisha, and I hope that she finds somebody that can relate to what she relates to. I'll take care of Moni financially, because I'm not a deadbeat-ass dad, but all that other shit is done. I know that five grand is more than enough to take care of a child per month. It's just that I know Taisha, and how she likes to shop, so I made sure I added some extra for the child in case her mother spends too much on herself.

I dry off, lotion up, and slip on my boxers, preparing to ease into bed. I slide under the cover behind Sasha and snuggle up under warmth. I kiss her softly on the back of the neck and drift off to sleep.

Morning came way to damn early for me; my headache was still there when I finally rolled over.

"Good morning, sleepy head," Sasha says while opening the blinds. The sunlight makes my head hurt even more. "What's wrong, you got a hangover?" she asks.

"Yeah," I answer, knowing damn well that alcohol ain't have shit to do with this headache. After a few moments Sasha nudges me awake, with something in her hand.

"Here, Baby, take this, it should make you feel better," she says, handing me a BC Powder and a cold Pepsi. That's why I love her so much, she's always looking out for me anyway she can.

"Thank you Boo," I tell her, allowing the nasty tasting powered substance to go down my throat. BC's were so damn nasty!

"You're welcome, Baby," she croons. "Breakfast is on the table when you're ready," Sasha informs me and then disappears out of the room. I lay back down. Twenty minutes later and after my headache subsides, I enter the kitchen and smile at my ladies.

"Hi, Daddy!" Raisha shouts with grits all over her mouth. Sasha and I sure made a gorgeous little girl.

"Hey. Rai-Rai, whatcha doing?"

"Eat eat, wit' Mommy," she tells me. I kiss her and Sasha on the cheek and prepare to dig in. The table is covered with food: French toast, bacon, sausages, scrambled eggs, biscuits, grits, home fries, and orange juice. Sasha don't be playing when it comes to breakfast, and my baby can burn.

After breakfast we all settle into the living room to make plans for the day. It wasn't Sunday but I had plans to spend time with my babies. I am bouncing Raisha on my knee, and she is laughing so hard that we are laughing right along with her. We are throwing ideas out about where we should go, and what we want to do, when we are interrupted by the doorbell. I hand Raisha to Sasha and go to answer the door. When I open it I am greeted by two white cops. One is short and fat, while the other one is tall and slim. I'm wondering why the Boys in Blue are at my house.

"Raimone Ford?" the short pudgy one asks.

"Yeah, that's me," I answer.

"You are under arrest for the kidnap and rape of Naitaisha Bolen," he announces.

Chapter Sixteen

Sasha

I don't know what the hell is going on. All I remember hearing is that Raimone is supposed to have kidnapped and raped somebody. He is handcuffed, and they are taking him toward their squad car. He keeps saying that he's innocent and for me to call Rob.

When I call Rob, he tells me that he'd take care of everything, and that he would call his lawyer right away. After hanging up with Rob, I still am not any closer to knowing anything, and I am very frustrated. I don't know what else to do, so I call Tasha.

"Hey Big Sis, Keisha and I were just talking about yo' ass," she says after she answers the phone.

"Tasha, I don't know what's going on," I cry out into the phone.

"What's wrong!" she yells.

"Raimone...he...he's... they took him to...to ja-ja-jail," I stammer as I continue to cry.

"What happened?" she asks, but I just keep crying. "Sasha, you gotta stop crying because I can't understand anything that you're saying," she says, trying to calm me down.

"The police came and got Raimone, talking about how he was under arrest because he...he...raped somebody." I sniffle, tears streaming down my face.

"Keish and I are on our way over there, okay, Sasha?" she promises.

"Ok, just use your key to come in," I tell her as I put down the phone. A half-hour later they are both coming in the door. I give them both hugs and we all sit down on the couch.

"Where's Rai?" they both ask in unison.

"I gave her a bath and put her to bed," I tell them. I explain to them what happened, and they are in awe, just like I am. The whole situation doesn't make any sense to me. I desperately need a drink. I get up and ask the girls if they want anything. Keish wanted a glass of Three Olives; Tasha wanted a glass of Grey Goose mixed with cranberry juice; while I opted for a glass of wine.

"I don't understand what the hell is going on here," said Keish.

"Me either," I solemnly replied. "All I know is that they said that he was to supposed to have kidnapped and raped somebody by the name of NaTasha or something like that." I didn't feel just yet the need to let them know that I had already had a clue as to who the girl was. I had to figure that part out myself first. We toss around different things that may have happened, and none of our conjectures made any sense. They end up spending the night in our guest room, because after more drinks, they are way too wasted to head home.

It's 6:30 Monday morning, and I'm about to walk out of the door to start my day. I am so pissed, due to the fact that I have yet to receive a call or anything from Raimone, and I have a migraine out of this damn world. I place Raisha in her car seat and drive off, headed to my parents' house. My dad is still working hard, while my mom is retired and looks after Raisha while I work.

It took me all of thirty minutes to get there, and I'm grateful that I have another hour before I have to be to work. I let myself in with the same key that I've had since I was a little girl, and notice that my mom is busy at the stove.

"There's Grandma's baby!" she says with a bright smile, as she turns around and reaches to take Raisha from my arms. I in turn hand her over, and give her a peck on the cheek. She sits Raisha in her highchair and goes back to making breakfast. "Since you got a little time, do you want something to eat?" she asks as she fixes her and Raisha's plates.

"No, Ma, I'm fine, I'm not really hungry," I answer listlessly.

"Not hungry? Now that's a first!" she laughs, but that stops abruptly when she notices that I'm serious.

"Is something bothering you, Sasha?" she asks.

"No, I'm fine," I say as tears stream down my face.

"Well you don't look fine to me, so tell me what's wrong," she asks, placing Raisha's bowl in front of her. She then pulls out two of the kitchen chairs, giving me the cue to have a seat.

"The police came to the house Saturday and took Raimone to jail, accusing him of rape. He told me that he's innocent, but I don't know what to do or believe!" I bawl. She hugs me and gently rubs circles in my back, like she did when I was little, in an attempt to calm me.

"Who is he supposed to have raped?" Mom asks.

"I don't know Ma, some girl," I lie. "They also said that he kidnapped her. I haven't talked to him since that day so I don't know what's going on."

"Well baby, I'm going to tell you like this. If he's innocent, he's innocent; God will make it right. There ain't nothing you can do, so stop stressing yourself out about something that's beyond your control. You have a baby to think about, and with Raimone being in jail, you are all she has," she points out, glancing over at Raisha. "So you dry your face, and do what you have to do for your child. I love Raimone like a son, but he's a grown man and he can take care of himself. You and your sister are grown, but y'all are still my babies. I'm not gonna stand around and watch you get broken down over something somebody else did."

"So you think he's guilty?" I ask, looking up at her.

"I'm not saying that," she answers. "What I am saying is something had to happen in order for him to be arrested, Sasha; you know that also."

She's right. I know something had to have happened; I just don't wanna believe it.

Getting up from the table, I go up the stairs and grab a rag from the linen closet. Closing the bathroom door behind me, I walk over to the mirror and look at my reflection.

"Snap out of it, Sasha; you can do it," I coach myself. Turning on the cold water, I wet the rag and place it on my face. I stay in the bathroom a little longer, fanning my face with my hands, trying to get rid of the puffiness around my eyes. When I'm satisfied I go back downstairs and into the kitchen.

"Do you feel better now?" Mom asks.

"A lot better," I tell her with a smile. That quick, my migraine was gone, and I was in a whole different mood. I thanked my mother, kissed her and Raisha on the cheek and left out for work.

The day went pretty well, considering how I felt when I woke up. I had a lot of appointments today, so that reason contributed to the day going by so fast. I finally go by my parent's house to get Raisha, thank Mom for the pep talk, and I'm on my way home. I'm not even in the house for five minutes when the phone rings; the caller ID says "Cuyahoga County Jail," so I know that it's Raimone.

"Hello," I answer.

"You have a collect call from Raimone who is in the Cuyahoga County Jail," I hear. "Press 1 if you wish to accept the charges," the recording says, and I dial 1 quickly.

"What the hell is going on, and why didn't you call me yesterday?" I ask before he has a chance to say a word. I take Raisha into her room and put on a Dora DVD to keep her busy for a little while.

"I have no clue Sash, this is bullshit!" Raimone says. "They didn't give me a chance to call yesterday; this is the only call they've giving me."

"What are they telling you?" I ask, as I make my way towards the living room.

"They ain't telling me shit. All they keep saying is that I'm accused of raping somebody," he says, sounding defeated. "I should be out of here within a couple of days, though, so I hope this situation will be straightened out soon."

"I'm not understanding. How is there a situation to begin with? Why the hell is some girl saying that you raped and kidnapped her?" I ask, because the shit isn't making any sense to me at all.

"I don't know what's going on my damn self, Sash, so I can't tell you much," he declares, but I don't believe shit he says. Like I said before, it makes no damn sense whatsoever! Plus when the officer's said the girl's name, I could tell by the look on his face that he knew who she was. "Whatever Raimone, so what's up?"

"Damn, Sash, what's your problem?" he asks, like he's irritated.

"Well first off, my husband is in jail for the rape and kidnapping of a bitch with the same name as the one you told me was your connect's sister. Second, you're acting like you have no clue what the fuck is going on. Third, you seem to have a damn attitude with me, because I'm frustrated! What the hell is wrong with you? Let me answer that one for you: You done lost your rabbit-ass mind, that's what's wrong!" I yell into the phone.

"Look, Sash, I'm trying to figure it all out myself. Just bear with me, please. All I can think of is the fact that she's mad that I don't fuck with her no more, so she's trying her best to sink me," he pleads.

"I'm gonna bear with you alright! When I ask you a fucking question, don't sit on the phone and act like you don't know what the hell I'm talking about! You knew it was her from the beginning, but you wanna play the dumb role with me and you want me to believe you? You're making it hard as hell for me to do that when you hold shit from me. Raimone, I am your wife, and if you can't keep it gutta with me, I don't know what to tell you. So I'm going to ask you again, if there's anything that you need to tell me, you better let it be known right motha fuckin' now. I'm not one for surprises, and that's all I've been getting lately. So put the shit out here, before I find out some other way, and that's all she wrote for you." I told him all this dead-ass serious. I'm tired of playing the guessing game with Raimone.

"Trust me, Baby, I don't know what the hell is going on. I haven't seen that girl since the night that she called the house, I swear," he begs. I want to believe him so bad, but I know it's a crock of shit.

"Well, in that case, listen closely because I'm only going to say this once. Don't fuck with me, Raimone, 'cause I promise you, you'll regret it," I inform him, and I mean every word that I say.

"I won't, baby, I just need for you to trust me," he replies hopefully.

"Well, you have it, don't stress about that," I say.

"You have one minute left for this call," the recording says, which prompts Raimone and I to begin to wrap up our call. He asks about Raisha, and before we know it, the recording is letting us know we have fifteen seconds left.

"Aight, Sash, Baby, I love you and I'll talk to you later," Raimone says.

"Ok, I love you too, Raimone. Bye," I told him as the call was disconnected. Even though I told Raimone that I completely trusted him, in my heart I knew it was something more—a lot more. I make Raisha and myself dinner, bathe us both, and went off to sleep to start yet another day.

Chapter Seventeen

Naitaisha

I wish I could've seen the look on Raimone's mug and his bitch's face when the police came to pick up his ass! I bet you he didn't even know I knew where he lived, but I fooled him. I'm no dumb bitch. Every time he leaves me in his car, I'm all in his shit. I know where they live, and Sasha's full name, because his car is registered to her. Shit, I even know the bitch's social security number, which I used to get me a few credit cards. Call me what you want to, I'm pretty sure you would do the same thing. I ain't gonna keep telling you not to fucking judge me!

Rinnnnnnnnnnnnng, Rinnnnnnnnnnnng...I glance at the caller ID and see the same number that has been popping up constantly since Saturday. Raimone has been blowing my phone up since they arrested his ass. He calls all day long, up until they cut the phones off; but I don't care, fuck him! He should've gotten the point by now; it's Tuesday and I have yet to answer the phone once. Shit, he didn't give a damn about me and my kid's feelings, so I don't give a damn about his freedom. I know I might sound crazy saying this, and honestly I really don't give a damn. If he thinks that he can play with my life like it ain't shit, and I can't have him, then nobody will.

I finally pulled myself together enough the following morning after crying my eyes out all night. I guess I got tired of feeling sorry for myself, so I decided to do something about it. I was not going to end up like my mother. I was not about to allow someone to just use me up and throw me away like garbage. I tried so damn hard to make it work with him, but he had plans of his own, I guess. Too bad those plans didn't include me, Moni, or our unborn child. Raimone was gonna pay for playing with my heart, and I was taking no prisoners.

I throw on a thin jogging outfit and head to my destination. I went "as is"; I didn't wash my ass or nothing, due to the fact that I was on a mission. I went to the 2nd district police station down the street to make a report. I sign in and wait in the lobby for close to twenty minutes before a young black officer comes to take my statement. He introduces himself to me as Officer Jackson, and he takes the seat across from me. Officer Jackson pulls out a pen and pad, and he advises me to start at any time.

I take a deep breath and I go on to tell him my story. I explain to him that Raimone and I were together for a couple of years, we had one child together and one on the way. I had just broken it off with him after recently finding out that he was married. I really loved Raimone and was feeling a little down lately due to our break up, so my girls invited me out to a night on the town. Even though I didn't really want to go, I obliged and ended up having pretty good time. That was, until I ran into Raimone and a couple of his friends. He was not too pleased with me, considering that I've been ignoring his telephone calls, so he flipped, forcing me out of the bar and into his car.

He drove me to my house, all the while telling me how ungrateful I was, and how he owns me. Once outside my house he climbed out and walked over to the passenger side, grabbed me by the neck and shoved me up the stairs. I show Officer Jackson the bruises on my neck and demonstrate the way he was doing me. I also gave him details of how I was raped for hours right inside of my home, in my bed, by someone who was supposed to love me. I put on an Oscar-winning performance and even throw in a couple of tears here and there to make it look even better.

Officer Jackson calls the ambulance and they took me to Metro, so that they could perform a rape kit. Because we didn't use condoms that night and I didn't bathe, his semen was still inside of me. I also had little tears inside of my vagina due to the sex being so rough, so that evidence backed up my rape story even more. They swabbed my insides, and he was immediately arrested. I told that boy not to fuck with me. Too bad he didn't listen.

Today I have a doctor's appointment at Metro in OBGYN at 11:30, so I decided to get my shower out of the way early. I slowly roll out of my bed and head toward the bathroom to get that task done. Today is my second ultrasound, and I'm anxious to find out if I'm having a boy or another girl. Once I feel that the temperature is right, I undress, step into the shower, and close the shower door. I allow the water to beat down on me for a couple of minutes, as it releases all the stress inside my body. I grab my rag and wash my body thoroughly, rinse, and turn off the water.

I step out, grab my towel, wrap it around my waist, and paddle into my bedroom. I sit down on the bed, and what do you know, Raimone is calling me once again. What the hell is he doing, calling me like that this early in the fucking morning anyways. I mean it ain't even nine yet! I can't ask him that because I ignore the shit out of it, and I proceed to rub my body down with lotion. After that task was done, I stroll into my walk-in closet to figure out my outfit for the day. Because it's a little windy outside, I opt for a soft pink summer dress, and low heel, open-toe sandals.

My stomach is growling. I head downstairs to make a bowl of Cocoa Puffs. I'm figuring that cereal should hold me over until after my doctor's appointment. Once I return back to my room, I grab a bottle of water and prop myself up on a few pillows. I then turn on the TV and finish watching my favorite movie of all time: Baby Boy. I love this movie so damn much, it's ridiculous. I know it word-for-word. Jody wasn't shit and Yvette knew it, but she stuck it out and ended up with her man in the end. That's what I thought would've happened between Raimone and me, until he fucked up my dreams. Thinking about his stupid ass, I almost missed my favorite part of the movie: the sex scene.

In this part, Jody comes over to the house talking

shit to Yvette, when he was in the wrong. Of course she knows this and puts his ass on blast. They get to causing a scene and arguing about hating each other, outside of the house. The scene instantly flips and they end up fucking like there was no tomorrow. I'm talking about straight fucking. Jody was all up in her and had her promising to clean up and make tacos. Jody silly ass does the "beat it up right" dance, and then the movie gets serious for a minute as they talk about Jody dying. After all of that, just as promised, Yvette is cleaning and making them damn tacos. I couldn't even laugh at her, 'cause that would've been me making them damn tacos, too.

I'm sitting here getting choked up, thinking about the arguments Raimone and I used to have and how we used to make up. I brush those tears aside. I can't let them stop me from what my plans are. Raimone did this to himself, and even though I love him, I gotta show him that I'm not to be fucked with. I have an hour before my appointment, so I hurry to get dressed so that I can make it on time. After getting myself together, I untie the scarf and let my red hair breathe. I shake my head a little bit so that my wrap instantly unravels. I finish the job with one of my wig brushes, grab a bottled water, and head out the door.

Pulling my truck into the garage up under the hospital, I park and walk toward the elevators. When I make it there, a man with the largest nose I've ever seen holds the doors for me, allowing me to get on with him. I almost want to say "never mind" because of the way he's looking at me, but I shut my mouth and step inside.

"How you doing?" Large Nose asks.

"Fine," I say, trying to be polite. I push number two, and the elevator goes up.

"Where yo' man at?" Now this nigga was really pushing his luck.

"Upstairs waiting on me," I lie.

Handing me a card, he says, "Why don't yo' fine ass take my number and call me when he's not around?" I start to go off, but I was saved by the bell, letting me know that I on the 2nd floor.

"I don't think that would be a good idea," I say tossing my red hair over my shoulder, as I step off the elevator and strut down the hall. I sign in and take a seat as I wait on the nurse to call my name.

Thirty minutes later I'm still in the same spot, uncomfortable as hell, due to me having to piss. My bladder is full because of all the water I was told to drink and my stomach is hurting. You would think that they would know that this would happen and call you as soon as you walk in the door, but that would be too much like right! A couple more minutes pass and I'm in the process of walking to the receptionist's desk to give her a piece of my mind when my name is called; boy, are they lucky.

"Good morning, Miss Bolen, how are you today?" the doctor says once I'm inside the room.

"Other than being full of water and having to piss bad as hell, I'm fine," I tell him, rolling my eyes. You should've seen the look on his mutha'fucka face, it was priceless.

I was ordered to pull my dress up past my belly and lay back on the table. The nurse covers my lower part of body with a white sheet, while the doc turns on the machine.

"This is going to be a little cold," he tells me, squirting a clear jell on top of my stomach. He rolls it around and in a matter of seconds my baby comes into view. "There he is."

"He?" I ask excitedly.

"Yes, you're having a bouncing baby boy," he informs me.

After printing me out a couple of pictures, he hands me some tissues and leaves out the room. I wipe the remaining jell off my stomach and head to the bathroom. I walk as fast as I can, but even that wasn't fast enough. No sooner than I pull my panties down, a stream of urine shoots out into the toilet bowl, causing me to groan; boy did that feel good. My legs were starting to cramp from squatting so long, due to me still pissing a full minute later. Rolling off some tissue, I wipe myself and flush the toilet with my foot.

Tossing the used napkin into the trash, I open the bathroom door, stepping out into the hallway. The ultrasound told me exactly what I'd hoped: I'm having a boy! I'm so excited I can't contain myself. I have to tell my girls. I stop in front of the elevator to call them, because I know that if I step inside, I'll lose signal.

"Hello," Big Pat says, sounding out of breath.

"What the hell were you doing?" I ask.

"Nothing, bitch, I had to run to the phone," she says.

"Hoe, you'se a mutha'fuckin lie. Yo' ass ain't ran no damn where!" I say, cracking up at my own joke.

"Fuck you! What the hell you want, anyways?" she says, and I can tell she's smiling.

"I can't tell you right now. Click over and call Tiff on three-way," I tell her.

"Hold on."

"Hello," Tiff answers.

"What's up, bitch?" I ask her.

"Shit, what's up with you hoes?" Tiff asks.

"Taisha's stanking ass wanna tell us something, that's why we're on three-way. So bitch, come on and spill it, got me over her all jittery n' shit!" Pat jokes

"I'm having a boy!" I shriek.

"Awwww shit!" Tiff yells.

"That's what I'm talking about! I betta be his damn godmother, 'cause Tiff's high-yellow ass got Moni," Pat states seriously.

"Fuck you with yo' fat ass!" Tiff yells back at Pat, and we all start to laugh. I then notice that people are starting to look at me like I am crazy for yelling and acting a fool in the hallway.

"Okay, bitches, I'm about to go into this cafeteria to get me something to eat, because I'm hungry as hell. I'm going to call you guys later," I tell them and disconnect the call.

After paying for my hoagie, Lay's plain chips, and bottled water, I start toward a table. I was in the process of pulling out my chair, when I saw something that made my blood boil.

Chapter Eighteen

Sasha

I spend my lunch break sitting in the cafeteria eating a tuna wrap and potato chips, talking to Tasha on the phone. We are laughing at the new guy she had just met a couple of weeks ago, Chris, and the fact that he was already saying the "L" word. Tasha sure did know how to pick these fall-in-love-fast type of dudes, and she treated them all the same: like shit. I was laughing so hard that I didn't notice that a woman was invading my space until she was standing directly in front of me.

"Can I help you?" I ask, because apparently she wanted something by the look on her face.

"You can't help me with shit, but I can damn sure help you," she says, rolling her neck, pointing directly at me.

"Do I know you?" I ask, trying desperately to keep my cool, all the while ignoring the hell out of Tasha yelling through the phone.

"No, I can't say that you do, but your husband knows me really well," she tells me. I tell Tasha that I will call her back, throw my phone in my purse and stand up, prepared for whatever home girl threw my way. I can't put my finger on it, but home girl looks really familiar.

"So what is it exactly that you want to say to me? It obviously must be pretty important for you to bring it to my place of employment," I say while giving this bitch the once over. She was a couple of inches taller than me and was slightly on the slimmer side. That fire red hair is what had me thinking that I knew this bitch from somewhere.

"Bitch, please! Don't flatter yo' self, 'cause wasn't nobody thinking about yo' ole' bum ass. I just came from my ultrasound appointment, saw you sitting here and decided to drop a line. Your husband and I have been together for a couple of years now, and we are expecting our second child," she informs me, pointing to the small bump under her shirt. "So can you do me a favor and tell Raimone that it's a boy?" she says, smirking.

"Since you know him so damn well, and you've been with him for years, why don't you tell him yourself?" I tell her. This bitch was working my nerves. I had to see where her head was. I had to see if she was serious or just a fucking hater.

"I would, but you can't make incoming calls to a jail cell. I guess he couldn't get enough of this good thing." She laughs thunderously, then squats pointing toward the middle of her legs. I swear I could feel the color instantly drain from my face. I can't believe this is the bitch that he was telling me about.

"What," she sneers, "you thought you were the only baby momma in his life?"

"Bitch, I'm far from a baby momma. I'm his wife," I flash my wedding ring in her face. "Apparently," I continue, "you couldn't hold that title, because if you could, we wouldn't be having this conversation."

"Wife? What the fuck do you get for being the wife? All you got is a dumb-ass piece of paper and a fucking ring! He bought you a house, he bought me a house. He buys you a car, I get a truck. He takes care of your bills, shit he takes care of mine, too. So I ask you again, what the fuck do you get for being the wife?" she asks loudly and I notice that we have an audience.

"Look, girl, I don't give a flying fuck about you or what he buys yo' nothing ass! I will tell you this, you need to get the hell out of here, causing a scene at my fucking job, or you will be sorry," I say as I step a little closer to her, all the while talking through my teeth.

"Bitch, ain't nobody scared of yo' dumb ass!" she yelled, spitting all in my face. The way she said the word bitch gave me the correct flash back and I suddenly know who this bitch is! She must of seen the change in my face, because she said, "Yeah, bitch, that was me who rocked yo' ass at the club."

I lost it and was in the process of knocking this bitch's head clean off her shoulders when a Metro off-duty Cleveland Police officer separated us. She continued to yell obscenities at me as he walked her down the spiral stairs and toward the exit. Even if I tried I couldn't describe how embarrassed I was at this moment.

About an hour later I was sitting in my supervisor's office, trying to explain that the incident was not my fault. I explain that I didn't even know who this woman was, and that I really tried to avoid the confrontation. I had witnesses to back up my story and everything, but to no avail. Even though I had been a great worker all those years, I was terminated due to the way that I behaved on the job; to say that I was pissed was a fucking understatement. The same security officer walked me to my locker like I was a fucking looney or something, and I have to fight to keep the tears from falling because I am so damn upset. I gather my belongings in a small box and walk out of Metro Health Medical Center as an RN for the last time.

So much was going through my mind on the drive to my mom's house to pick up Raisha. I grab all of her things, place them in her book bag, and head home. I didn't stay around talking like I usually did because I didn't want to break down in front of my mom. How could I explain that my husband has been cheating, about to have two children with his mistress, and was in jail for the kidnap and rape of this same female? You're right—I couldn't think of a way either, and that's why I was on my way home.

I pull up in the McDonalds drive-thru and order Raisha a cheeseburger Happy Meal, because considering what I had been through, I wasn't in a cooking mood. Tasha had been calling my phone nonstop since the time that we had talked at lunch earlier, but I didn't feel like talking to anybody so I didn't answer. After Raisha ate, I gave her a bath, put on her pajama's, and put her down for bed. I lit the candles that were around my jetted tub and ran myself a nice hot bubble bath because I needed to relax. I let out a sigh as I slipped into the hot water and let my mind wander free. An hour later I was relaxed, washed, and in my bed staring at the ceiling, wondering what in the hell I was going to do. I loved my job and for a bitch to just walk in and take that from me at the drop of a dime was beyond me.

When I step out of the tub, my house phone rings instantly; it's Tasha. I felt kind of bad for ignoring her, because I know that she was more than likely worried to death about me, so I answer.

"Hello," I say slowly.

"Where the fuck you been all day? I've called yo' ass bout a hundred times and you just now decide to answer?" she asks, and I can tell that she's highly upset.

"I'm sorry, sis, but you wouldn't believe the day that I have had," I tell her, preparing to fill her in on my drama.

"That's the reason why I've been calling so damn much! The last time we talked, some woman was in your face talking reckless; that's the last I heard from you. Then I call the hospital and they tell me you no longer work there. What the fuck is going on?" she demands to know.

"They were right, I don't work there anymore. I was fired today."

"What!" she yells, incredulous.

"The woman that you heard me talking to earlier is supposedly Raimone's baby mother. She's also the same girl from the club whom I was fighting with a couple of weeks ago," I inform her.

"Wait a minute, Sasha, I don't get it," she says.

"Shit, I don't either," I explain, exhausted. "But apparently she'd just come from getting an ultrasound and saw me sitting at the table and came over. She told me that she's been with him for a few years, and they are expecting their second child, which she just found out is a boy. She knew Raimone was in jail and everything Tash—she's the reason he's in there. This shit isn't making any sense to me. What the hell is going on?" I blubber to her, as if my twin could answer the questions that I didn't even have the answers to.

"I don't know, Sasha, I honestly don't know. If this shit is true, I wouldn't feel no sympathy for Raimone because he's a dirty mothafucka. That would explain why ole' girl wanted to kick yo' ass that night; that would explain a lot. Remember, we couldn't figure out why she was so mad about a little bump. Come to find out it wasn't about the bump at all," Tasha surmises.

"This shit is crazy, man, I don't know what the hell is going on but I'm damn sure gonna get to the bottom of it," I say wearily. I explain to her that I'm tired. We wrap up our conversation with a promise to talk early in the morning.

I rest in my bed and cry from deep in my soul. It amazes me how things are turning out. Here I thought my life was perfect, but I guess nobody's is. My shit is in shambles and I didn't even know it. Here I am at home being the "good wife" and my husband was running around town with some stank hoe making babies. I cry and cry until I can't cry anymore. After hours of this same routine, I promise myself that this would be the last time that I'd shed one tear over Raimone LaShawn Ford.

Chapter Nineteen

Raimone

I swear when I get out of this bitch, I'm gonna fuck Taisha's ass up! She knows damn well that I ain't kidnapped or raped her dumb ass! I've been in jail for four days on a bunch of bullshit, and my back is against the wall. I go to court in the morning and hopefully they let me up outta here. I'm so fucked right now, it don't make sense! Something told me not to even fuck with her that night, but I ended up feeling sorry for her retarded ass. I fell right into her trap, 'cause she damn sure seduced me with that fake-ass "I'm drunk" act.

My lawyer, Antony "Tony" Peterson, came to see me today, and I'm not at all pleased with what he had to say. He was a close friend of mine and Rob's so it was nothing for us to call him when we were in a bind.

Tony was a damn good lawyer, and I trusted him whole heartedly. Just looking at him you would think he was a regular white guy, with blonde hair, blue eyes, and a serious tan. The so-called "serious" tan was actually not a tan at all, it was compliments of his Caucasian mother and African father. Standing an inch or two taller than me, with the build of a basketball player, he had the swagger of a black guy in a white boy's body. Tony told you like it was, he didn't sugarcoat shit and that is what I liked about him. That was the case when he told me everything I was charged with, and what I was looking at. He informed me that she told the police everything about our whole situation, and that it's not looking good for me at this moment.

"She told the police that you saw her at the bar and forced her into your car. What the fuck happened, Raimone?" he asks me, once I am seated in the visitation room.

"She told me that she didn't have a ride home because her and her girls got into it. She was leaning on the hood of my car crying and shit, so I gave her a ride," I explain to him, leaning back in the chair, running my hands through my hair.

"She also states that she told you multiple times that she didn't want to have sex with you, and that it was over," Tony says.

"Man, that bitch lying!" I exclaim as I slam my hands down on the table. "She's been calling my phone non-stop since I stopped talking to her ass! I can show you the text messages and everything, man. She got this shit twisted! When I took her home, she was the one that went down on me, sucking my dick and shit!" I yell, not giving a fuck because this bitch is really trying to sink me. "Come on, Tony, why in the fuck would I rape her if I've been fucking her for years?" I ask.

"I know you didn't rape that damn girl, Raimone, but I'm neither the prosecutor nor the judge. She's not denying any of that, but she is telling them that she broke it off about a month ago after she found out that you were married. I ain't even gonna front; her story is looking pretty good," he informs me with a look of sympathy in his eyes.

"I'm gone kill that bitch when I get outta here!" I shout so loud that the guard walks to the door to make sure everything thing is alright. Tony holds his hand up to let them know that we're cool and they go back about their business. I should kill my own damn self for being so dumb about this whole situation.

I remember her telling me that if I continued to hurt her, that there was no telling what she might do. Now I fully understand what she meant, because she threw me through a loop with this one. Tony also went on to explain to me that I was facing two felony one's, and up to twenty in prison. If convicted, I would also have to register as a sex offender once I was released. I couldn't have that, especially for some shit that I didn't do. Taisha better stop with the bullshit, I swear. I've been calling her ass since I got locked up, and she hasn't answered yet. I know she knows it's me, cause who in the hell else would be calling from county? I gotta get in contact with her in some kind of way to make her drop these damn charges. Something's gotta shake.

Tony promises me that he's going to do anything in his power to poke holes in her story, and that he's gonna make sure I get a bond tomorrow at court. After my visit is up, I gather my things and head down to take a quick shower. I call Sasha after I'm done, and my already fucked-up situations gets a lot worse.

"Hello," she greets me tentatively, after she accepts the charges.

"Hey, Baby," I say.

"Hey," she replies.

"How was your day?" I ask.

"Well other then getting fired yesterday, it went pretty well." She says this as if getting fired was nothing. Sasha loves her job, so I'm confused.

"Fired?" I ask, shocked.

"Yes, fired, and you wanna know why, Raimone?" she says testily.

"Yeah, I wanna know, why would they fire you, Baby?" I ask, confused as to why she would ask me, of all people.

"Well I got fired because your Baby Momma came up to my damn job acting a damn fool!" she shouts so loudly into my ear that I have to temporarily pull the phone away.

"Baby Momma? What are you talking about, Sasha?" I ask, as I feel myself getting sick to my stomach. This can't be happening!

"Don't play me for stupid, Raimone. You know damn well who and what I'm talking about. The bitch you supposedly raped, which is also the same bitch who you told me was your connect's sister. She told me all about yall's lil relationship and the fact that you have a child and one on the way. Oh yeah, she also told me to tell you that she's expecting a boy, which she found out today during her ultrasound. So what do you have to say for yourself, Mr. Ford?"

"Baby, don't believe that bullshit. That bitch's lying!

She's trying to do anything in her power to fuck up my life, because I don't fuck with her anymore. The bitch is crazy, Sash! I know I was wrong for the way I played my hand, but I swear to you, that girl is lying," I declare, trying to get her to believe me. It feels as if the air is being sucked from my lungs as I'm struggling to breathe. I'm getting nauseous thinking about Sasha leaving me. "I never even fucked that girl, so if she is pregnant, it's by another nigga," I lie.

"How you sound, Raimone!" Sasha says. "Asking me to believe you, when you lied to me from the jump? You told me that she was skinny as hell, and funny looking. This bitch wasn't all that skinny, and "funny looking" isn't the way I'd describe her. You are a fucking liar, Raimone, and I ain't got time for you or your bullshit! Then I come to find out that this is the same bitch who swung on me at the club awhile back. So this hoe knew what I looked like and everything. This shit is going way too far, if you ask me! Then you gonna tell me that you didn't fuck her—but she's supposed to be pregnant with your child. Not only is she claiming to be pregnant with your baby, but also she says that you two have a child already. What the fuck is wrong with you?" she screeches loudly in my ear.

"Baby, please believe me, that girl is lying because she wants what you have. I can't live without you. I promise that I'll make this right when I get out of here tomorrow, I promise you. I'm going to kill that bitch for putting us through this un-necessary bullshit!" I tell her, and I'm dead serious about it.

"Naw, nigga, apparently this shit is necessary, and it's all your fucking fault!" Shasha admonishes. "Don't you sit here and blame somebody else for the shit you've done. Don't you dare put the blame on nobody but your damn self, because you caused all of this. She couldn't do anything that you didn't give her the power to do, so lay in that bed yo' ass made," she demanded.

"I know, Sasha. I know I'm the one to blame. I'm just asking you to stick it out with me, and you'll see that I'm telling the truth. Please don't walk away from me, baby, I need you. I'll be home tomorrow, and I promise I'll make this right," I cried into the phone. I couldn't lose my family behind this bullshit, I just couldn't.

"What you need to do is get your shit together, that's what you really need to do. This shit here ain't got nothing to do with me. So you and your bitch keep me and my daughter out of this. I gotta go," she says and hangs up before I get a chance to reply.

I say to myself as I head back to the cell, "I gotta get the hell outta here, man, I'm really gonna fuck Taisha's grimy ass up for real now."

I have murder on my mind.

Chapter Twenty

Naitaisha

"Bitch, you are sick!" Pat roars in my ear later that
night after I tell her and Tiff what happened. I tell them
about me falsely accusing Raimone for rape, and that
he was locked up for it. Pat was cracking up, saying that
Raimone got what he deserved for playing games, while
Tiff was unusually quiet.

"I could've bought that bitch for a dollar when I told
her that we were having a boy this time!" I giggle as I
sit on my bed with a green apple and knife. I've been
craving green apples since I've been pregnant.

"What happened after you told her that?" Pat asks
excitedly.

"That bitch tried to swing on me, but security stepped
in. I was kinda salty 'cause I was gonna let her knock the

shit outta me. Then I was gonna take my ass downtown and press charges on her dumb ass for assault. You should've seen her face when she realized that I was the same chick from the club! I think she even got fired, because I waited outside for awhile and saw her come out with a small box in her hand," I laugh hysterically, while cutting off a piece of the apple and placing it into my mouth.

"I know that had to fuck her up," Tiff says seriously, finally joining in on the conversation. "I would've been trying to kill yo' ass too. You already fucking her husband, got two kids by him, and you steal on her at the bar. You're fucking up her family, and she's pissed! What did you expect the woman to do, invite you over to dinner?" Tiff says.

I wasn't going to bite my tongue.

"Shut the fuck up, Tiff, you act like it's your husband or some shit! Bitch, you taking up for her like you know her! If you got something to say, go on ahead and say it, hoe, don't beat around the motha fuckin bush!" I challenge her.

"You shut the fuck up, Taisha, with yo' grimy ass! I ain't gotta know her to know that the shit is wrong. You mad at her cause her husband won't leave her, and that shit ain't right!" she asserts adamantly.

"Okay, okay, both of y'all calm down, it's not that serious. We're girls, we shouldn't even be arguing about shit like this," Pat intervenes.

"Naw, Pat, fuck that. Let the bitch say what she has to say. Go head, Tiff, you got something on your chest that you wanna get off, now's the time," I goad her.

"First of all, I ain't taking up for nobody. I'm just saying that it's fucked up, flat out! We are sitting on the phone laughing and joking about ruining that girl's life. You and I both know that if it happened to one of us, it wouldn't be funny. I just think the shit is going too far, and you betta stop while you can. You know I love you and Moni to death, but this here ain't a game, Taisha," she sighs. "You fucking with that man's freedom by putting him in jail for a crime that he didn't commit. Then you approach his wife at her job to try to break up his home, and in the process you get her fired. I'm not saying that you're the only wrong party in this because you're not, he's just as much to blame. I'm just saying that you're going about it the wrong way. You gotta know that when he gets out he's going to come for you. I just don't want to see you get hurt behind this, that's all I'm saying," Tiff finishes, and it sounds like she's crying, but I can honestly give a fuck less.

"That's the problem, Tiffany. I don't need you to worry about me or Moni because we are gonna be just fine. So you can save you pity-party for the next bitch, because this one can handle her own. Call me later Pat, I'm about to take a bath and lay down," I say as I end the call. Who the fuck does Tiff think she is? She does the same shit I do and doesn't give a damn about people's feelings. The bitch is a fucking hypocrite, and I don't need that kind of person in my life.

It's been two days since me and Tiff got into it, and I have yet to talk to her since then. I just got off the phone with Pat and she's telling me that we need to squash our beef, but I'm trying not to hear it. I tell Pat that I just can't understand how Tiff thinks I'm wrong for what I've done, when I'm the victim here. I'm the one stuck raising two kids on my own, while they are off living the life of a happy family. If Raimone didn't want to be with me, he should have told me years ago. Instead he continued to come around and made broken promises, knowing that he'd never follow through with them. So for that he has to pay, and if a long prison term is his payment, so be it. Pat agrees and tells me that she'll bring pizza and Pepsi when she comes by later, and we hang up.

The prosecutor calls to warn me that Raimone made bail, and that he should be walking out of the jail at any moment. He also informs me that if he comes anywhere near me, to call the police immediately. I assure him that I will do just that and I dial my mom's number.

"Good afternoon," she pleasantly answers.

"Hey, Mom," I say.

"Hello, Naitaisha. How are you, Baby?" she asks.

"I'm doing fine. Where's Moni?" I ask.

"She's watching cartoons, hold on a sec," she says as she calls out to Moni.

"Hey, Mommy," my Angel says.

"Hey, baby, whatcha doing?" I ask as I dump the core of the apple I just demolished into my bathroom garbage. I run the plate and knife under some water and place them temporarily in the bathroom sink.

"Eating noodles and watching cartoons with MaMa," she tells me. "Are you coming over here?" she asks in her innocent little voice.

"Not today, Moni, but I'll be over to see you tomorrow, I promise," I say. But there is no response from Moni, so I say, "Hello?" but I get no answer.

My mom gets back on the phone. "Naitaisha, you have to get yourself together, child," my mom scolds. I'm guessing Moni is mad because I'm not coming over and gave the phone back to my mother. "I love

Moni, and she's more than welcome to stay here with me forever if you need her to. If that is the case, then we can sign her over immediately. You're having another baby and you're not taking care of the one you've got. I'm going to tell you right now that I'm not taking care of that other one. That's between you and the father."

"I didn't call to ask you to take care of my baby, Mom." I say, irritated.

"You also didn't ask me to take care of Moni," she reminds me. "You just dropped her off and never came back. Now I'm not going to talk you to death, I'm just speaking my peace. Anyways, what do you plan on doing for her birthday? It is next week."

"I know her birthday is next week, I did give birth to her," I retort smartly. "I'm not sure what I'm going to do just yet, but I'll talk to you later. Give Moni a kiss for me," I tell her and disconnect the call. I get tired of constantly hearing that I need to get my life together. My life is together. I'm going to show her and everybody else that Naitaisha Latriese Bolen can take care of herself! I'm going to go back to school and get a job. I don't need a man in my life to feel whole. I can do this shit by my damn self! You just wait and see, I'm going to show them.

Ding………..dong.

The doorbell interrupts my thoughts. Probably Pat with the food. I snatch the door open.

It's Raimone.

"What the hell are you doing here?" I ask Raimone as I stand in the doorway with one hand on my hip, the other on the door. I'm scared as hell, but I'm not going to let him know that. "I asked you a question, what the hell are you doing here?" I ask again, rolling my neck;

but instead of replying, he attacks me. He grabs me by my neck, slamming me against the closet opposite the front door with all of his might. He shuts the door and walks over to me, and I almost piss on myself when I notice the look in his eyes: death.

He lifts up his leg and stomps me on the floor like I was his worst enemy.

"Raimone, stop!" I cry out, but to no avail. He continues to kick and stomp me viciously. My house phone rings, and Raimone is temporarily distracted. That gives me just enough time to get up and run. Racing up the stairs with Raimone on my heels, I make it into my bathroom with just enough time to close and lock the door.

"Bitch, I'm gonna kill you!" Raimone shouts as he bangs on the closed door.

"Please stop, what about the baby? I'm pregnant with your son, Raimone." I plead, hoping he's going to come to his senses and calm down.

"I don't give a fuck about no damn baby. I told you not to play with me, Taisha. Yo' stupid ass put me in jail for no fucking reason, and you're trying to ruin my family. Bitch, I'm gonna kill you!" he yells, pounding on the door once again.

"I'm sorry, Mone. I'll drop the charges tomorrow — I swear! I made a mistake. I love you, Baby, and can't live without you. Please stop!" I beg, but apparently he isn't fazed because he continues to bang and kick on the door. I know that the door is going to cave at any moment, so I search frantically for something to protect myself with. After rummaging around for a weapon, my eyes instantly land on the knife in the sink that I'd used earlier to cut my apple. I grip it with all of my might, ready to hurt Raimone if I have to. The door flies open, slamming against the wall. I brace myself as he rushes me like a raging bull. I swing the knife with full force, but he blocks it and grabs a hold of my wrist. I see stars as he slams me against the wall, placing the arm that still holds the knife high above my head.

"Bitch, you trying to stab me?" he asks, spitting directly into my face.

"I wasn't going to stab you," I lie, wishing that I'd hit my mark.

"Lying bitch!" he yells, twisting my arm until I cry out in pain and drop the knife.

"I should slice yo' fucking throat right now!" he says after he picks up the knife and places it under my neck with enough force to break the skin. I feel a small amount of blood trickle down my neck and onto my shirt, and I am so fucking scared. I start to think that maybe I did take it too far with all of the things that I was doing to him.

"Raimone, I'm sorry for everything that I've done," I say, trying to make one last plea, hoping that he'll stop this attack. I am fearful that if this continues, my son isn't going to make it.

"Shut the fuck up!" he roars, drops the bloody knife and slaps me so hard it feels like my face is on fire. I fall like a rag doll and hit my head against the toilet bowl. Raimone grabs hold of my hair and drags me from the bathroom into my bedroom, giving me carpet burns on my back and legs in the process.

"Bitch," he says, "you think you so smart, don't you?" He kicks me once in the stomach.

"Raimone, please stop!" I cry out.

"You didn't think to stop when you were pressing

those bogus-ass charges on me, was you? Or when you went to my wife's job and got her fired!?" he yells, kicking me in the stomach after every question. He then kneels down and places his hands around my neck and squeezes tightly. I start to think about my kids and how I have to live for them, and I realize that I have to do something. I reach out and dig my nails as deep into his face as I can, trying to get him off me. He pries my hands away as the blood flows from the open cuts in his face. He punches me so hard in my eye that it instantly swells closed. I try to scream out from the intense pain in my eye, but I can't—I don't have enough air in my lungs. Putting his hands back around my neck, he goes back to strangling me. I feel myself slipping in and out of consciousness. I can't fight it anymore, and everything goes black.

Chapter Twenty-One

Raimone

I drive home in a zone. My mind is all over the place at this moment, and I'm not even sure what I've done. I hope the police aren't at my house waiting for me when I get there, because I don't need that right now. I haven't been out on bond for two hours and already I've put myself in deep shit. I walked out of County on a mission. I went to the crib to grab my car and headed right over to Taisha's house to handle my business. I didn't even head in to see Sasha, or my Raisha; I had shit to do. I admit that I went over there to fuck her up, but when she opened the door with that stank-ass attitude, I lost it. I mean she put me in jail on some bogus shit, and got the audacity to play the fuck outta crazy!

That all changed as soon as I started to put my foot

in her ass. The part that killed me was when she started talking about the baby, like that was gonna make me stop doing her dirty. Truth be told I didn't give a fuck about her or the baby, because of the way that she played her hand. She ain't give a fuck about the baby when she was up at Sasha's job, all in her face, talking reckless, trying to start a damn fight.

I pull up at my house wondering what I'm going to be confronted with. I haven't talked to Sasha since the night before, and I really don't know what to expect. I'm thinking how I'm going to explain why I looked the way I did. My face is scratched up like I got into a fight with a caged animal, and there's blood all over my neck and shirt. I can't do anything but tell the truth, and hope that Sasha understands my reasoning. I promised my mother that I would always protect my family and never let anyone disrespect them, and I was keeping that promise. I let Taisha slide with too much shit, and I think she'd gotten comfortable fucking me over. This time she went too damn far. You don't fuck with a man's family or his freedom, and she did both.

I walk into the dark house and notice that Sasha and Raisha aren't home, which is good because I can clean myself up before they arrive. I take off my clothes, put them in a plastic bag, and toss them into the garbage can. I grab everything that I need for the task at hand and hop in to the shower. My face throbs as the hot water hits the deep cuts with no remorse. I groan from the pain, but I continue to stand under the flow and allow the blood that's caked up on my face to go down the drain. After cleaning up, I dab my face with a cotton ball full of peroxide and think about how I'm going to get out of this mess.

Chapter Twenty-Two

Sasha

I finally walk into the house at around 2 a.m. and there isn't a light on. I know Raimone's home because his car's parked in the driveway. I know for sure it was in the garage earlier when I left. It's funny because I'm wondering how long he's been out of jail, and how come he hasn't attempted to contact me at all today. I sigh and push those thoughts to the back of my mind, because more than likely he had to make up with his bitch. If that is the case, then I hope he takes his shit and goes to live with her, because I damn sure ain't sharing a man. I don't give a damn who he is and how much money he has.

Once inside the house I remove my jacket and place it and my purse on the couch. Tip-toeing into my bedroom, I observe Raimone, sleeping. He's so out of it that he doesn't even feel my presence in the room. Quietly I grab pajamas, underclothes, and toiletries for the shower. I stroll to the guest bathroom, stopping in the hall to grab a towel and two rags out of the linen closet. I close and lock the guestroom door, because this is where I will be sleeping tonight. Picking up the phone, I call to let Tasha know that I've made it home safely, and to kiss Raisha for me. After a couple of minutes we disconnect the call and I run and test my shower water.

Standing in front of the mirror, I pull my hair on top of my head and secure it with a clamp, then lightly apply Noxzema to my face. Turning on the faucet I select the temperature that is right for me and splash just enough water to remove the facial cream. Using one of the rags, I blot my face to remove the excess water that is dripping down to my shirt. I then undress, climb into the running shower and slide the door closed. The water attacks my body in such a way that I can't help but whimper. After my shower is finished, I dress, climb underneath the covers and drift into a peaceful sleep.

A soft knock on the door awakens me from dreamland and I know it's only one person.

"Yes, Raimone," I say.

"Baby, why you in here?" he says.

"I'm in here because this is where I want to be," I answer with an attitude.

"Well can you open up the door so I can talk to you?" he asks, and when I don't reply, he begs, "Please, Sasha?"

I sluggishly saunter to the door and unlock it. As he enters, I'm already climbing back into bed.

"What happened to your face, Raimone?" I ask.

Instantly my attitude is gone when I see the deep cuts in his face. I gasp at how painful it looks as he sits down on the bed, and I tenderly touch one of the numerous cuts.

"Do you really wanna know?" he asks, and instantly my attitude comes back. I use my right foot to kick him with all my might off the bed and onto the floor. "Get the fuck out, Raimone!" I shout.

"No, Baby, it's not what you think," he stammers.

"So that bitch didn't scratch your face up like that?" I ask, cutting him off.

"Well, yeah, it is what you think, but I have a good reason for all of this," he promises as he stands up and grabs hold of my hands. "I made everything right."

"What do you mean?" I ask, because I don't know how that could be.

"I told you I was going to make sure that everything is alright with us, and that's exactly what I did. You don't have to worry about that bitch fucking with us or our family ever again."

"What did you do, Raimone?" I ask seriously.

"All you need to know is, I took care of that situation and we can put all of this bullshit behind us now," he says.

"Did you hurt that girl?" I inquire, afraid of what the answer would be.

"I'm not going to go into it. The less you know, the better. Just know that she will no longer be able to cause us anymore pain. I love you, Sasha, with everything in me, and I'd die if I ever lost you. I know I fucked up and I can't be mad at you if you decide to give me shit for the next five years. I will do anything in my power to make this right and to be a good father and husband to you and Raisha. All I ask is that you give me a chance to show you," he says sincerely, holding my hand.

"Raimone, I love you, but I don't know what to say right now. This is so overwhelming and I honestly don't know whether I'm coming or going. Can you just give me time to get my thoughts in order?" I ask, with tears in my eyes.

"I respect that, Sash, and I'm here whenever it is that you want to talk." He walks toward the door. "Just know that I'm not going to give up on us, and I hope that you're not going too, either." And with that, he left. I pull the cover over my head and rested there, thinking about everything that had transpired within these past few weeks.

I finally climb out of bed a few hours later with an intense urge to pee. After I wipe myself, I turn on the water in the sink, apply paste to my toothbrush and proceed to brush my teeth. My mouth is fresh, my face is washed, and I'm on my way into the kitchen to make something quick to eat. I hear Raimone on the phone with somebody and the closer I get to the kitchen, the clearer his conversation is.

"Rob, man, that bitch tried to pull the skin off my face with her damn nails," he says, and instantly my ears perk up to hear the story. I slow down my pace so that he doesn't know that I'm awake and in the vicinity. He continues his conversation. He went on to describe the way that he was beating her, and imitating the way she was crying and screaming. The whole conversation made me sick to my stomach and I couldn't take it anymore, so I cleared my throat to make my presence known.

"Hey, Rob, let me call you back in a lil while, man,"

Raimone says. Obviously Rob agrees and Raimone closes his cell phone. "Hey baby, you finally woke up, I see," he says with a smile and I cringe at the scratches and gashes on his face. "It's that bad, huh?" he asks, noticing the look on my face.

"Actually, it is," I reply and walk by him into the kitchen. Opening the fridge, I glance inside to see what catches my eye as a quick snack. Gripping the handle on the milk, I decide that my meal will consist of cereal. I grab a bowl and spoon out of the dishwasher, sit them both on the island, and then I head to the pantry to grab the box of Peanut Butter Crunch. Because I really don't want to be around Raimone, I decide to eat my bowl of cereal inside the kitchen.

An hour later I'm dressed in light blue jean capris, a white screen tee that has "Cute as a Button" in pink across the chest, with a picture of a button on it. On my feet is a pair of white Air Maxx. The pink shoestrings and Nike check on the side of them match the pink in my shirt. I grab my colorful Dooney and Burke purse and prepare to head out of the door.

"Where you 'bout to go?" Raimone asks as I walk past him on the couch.

"Out," I said shortly, to let him know that it was none of his damn business.

"Well, I guess I'll see you later, cause I'll be here all day," he replies.

"That's fine. See ya," I say to him as I close the door behind me. It's a beautiful day outside and the sun is shining brightly. I hit the button and the top of my Sebring instantly glides back into its position as I turn up "Go Head" by Gucci: "Shawty got an ass on her, Uh huh. I'm a put my hands on her, Uh hu. I'm a spend a couple grads on her, Uh huh. I'm a pop a rubber band on her, Uh huh." I bob my head and sing along as I pull out of my driveway and to my destination.

The wind feels wonderful in my hair as I pull up to the ATM at First Merit bank. After withdrawing my cash, I'm on my way to Tasha's house. I call her from my cell phone to inform her that I'm on my way, because she's slow as hell. Fifteen minutes later I pull up in front of her house, hit my alarm and head in the direction of her apartment. After climbing the stairs to the second floor, I knock lightly on the door.

"Who is it?" Tasha asks.

"Bitch, it's me!" I yell, knowing damn well she knew it was me. She opens the door laughing and I push my way past her with a fake attitude and sit on the couch. "Rai Rai!" I shout, calling out to Raisha.

"Girl, she sleep! I laid her down for a nap awhile ago and she hasn't woke up yet. Go wake her up, 'cause it's about time she woke up anyways, with her lil lazy ass," Tasha explains to me with a smile.

I get off the couch and head into the room decorated especially for Raisha. If I didn't know any better I'd think she lived here instead of with me. The room had an all-white bed with a canopy. The sheets and comforter were Dora the Explorer. The walls had Dora and Boots stickers, and the floor had a big pink fluffy rug on it. My baby looked so peaceful under the covers that I almost didn't want to wake her. I gently nudge her and she continues to snore lightly. I apply a little more force and she slowly opens her eyes. Once she's focused she instantly says "Mommy" and wraps her arms around my neck. I pick her up and carry her into the bathroom to brush her teeth and wash her face.

"Hey, Baby, did you miss me?" I ask her as I squeeze a little bit of toothpaste out of the tube. Raisha smiles and nods her head up and down, letting me know that she did.

"Say ahhhh," I tell her, and she opens her mouth so that I can proceed to brush her teeth. After I wash her face, we head back into the living room to join Tasha, who is watching "Girlfriends." I join her on the couch with Raisha on my lap, because it is one of my favorites. It's the episode when Toni is depressed because her boyfriend Gregg left her out of the blue, and she doesn't know why. Joan feels bad because she is the reason why Gregg left Toni, due to the fact that she slipped up and told him that Toni was going to break up with him, which she wasn't.

Well, anyways, Joan ends up taking Toni to the Sinbad Music Festival so that they can unwind, and hopefully so that Toni could get out of the funk that she was in. The good thing is that Toni does just that, but not the way that Joan expects. Toni comes in the next morning flashing her rock and lets her know that she agreed to marry and live with the football star that she met the night before. Joan doesn't know what to do, so she reluctantly tells Toni why Gregg broke up with her—big mistake! Toni smacks the shit out of Joan, and it takes Mya and Lynn to pull Toni off Joan. Toni grabs her things and storms out of the hotel room, and Joan heads home only to walk in on Toni trying to sleep with her boyfriend on her couch.

"I would've beat the brakes off that bitch for real!" Tasha exclaims and I can't do nothing but laugh.

"You always wanna fight somebody, with yo' violent ass!" I say.

"Get the fuck outta her, Sash," Tasha admonishes me. "Yo' ass just as violent as I am. So you mean to tell me, if yo' girl did you like that, you wouldn't do shit?" she asked, already knowing the answer.

"Hell naw, I'd have fucked her grimey ass up!" I smile, proving her point. We sit around and watch TV for a little while longer before Keish calls and we all decide to head to Longhorn for dinner. It was a great meal.

"Man, that steak was good as hell," Tasha exclaims, licking her lips.

"Hell, yeah, I am full as hell right now," Keish declares, throwing her head back and rubbing her flat stomach in a circular motion.

"Y'all both ain't never lied, 'cause I am so full, I'm damn near sick!" I say and we all crack up laughing. I pay the tab, and all take a peppermint from the hostess stand as head out of the door. I grab hold of my baby's hand as we cross the parking lot, headed to Tasha's Silver 2005 Chevy Tahoe. Keish places the straps over Raisha's shoulders, and I hop into the passenger seat.

"You gotta work tomorrow, Tasha?" Keish asks.

"Naw, I'm off tomorrow," Tasha answers.

"I ain't gotta work either," I say, trying to be funny.

"I know yo' ass ain't gotta work, Sasha, wit yo' silly ass! What's up, though? Y'all trying to get fucked up tonight?" she asks.

"Hell yeah!" Tasha and I say in unison.

"Shit. Well, we betta head to the liquor store now, 'cause it'll be closing soon," Keish says.

We all walk in different directions inside of the liquor store, as we searched for what we each wanted. Tasha selects a bottle of Grey Goose, Keish grabs Three

Olives, and I get a small pint of Hennessy. Keish pays for all of the drinks, and we pile back into Tasha's truck. We stop at a store to grab orange juice, cranberry juice, Pepsi, chips, and some other snacks before retiring to Tasha's. Raisha was knocked out by the time we pulled up, so I unbuckle her from her carseat and carry her upstairs. I walk her into her room, take off her clothes and place her in the bed. After tucking her in, I plant a kiss on her forehead and crack the door on my way out.

Chapter Twenty-Three

Raimone

It's 5:30 a.m. and I'm sitting in the house, pissed that Sasha has yet to bring her ass home. I'm really salty because I can't even call and trip on her about it, considering the situation I'm in. I mean damn, she could've called and said something, especially because I let it be known that I was gonna be home all day. She did tell me that she needed time to herself, and I'm trying to respect her wishes. I just hope that she's not spending her time with another nigga, 'cause even though I did what I did, I couldn't take that. I just can't picture someone else touching my wife the way I touch her, or making her smile the way I used to. Just thinking about it right now gets me over here ready to kill something!

Isn't it crazy the way men think? I mean, we can

cheat on our women and fuck all of the chicks we want, but if we even think our girl is doing anything like that, we flip the fuck out! I can't really explain the logic, but I kinda got a clue as to what it's all about and actually it's very simple. We don't tie sex to emotion like women. In fact, we can fuck three girls in one day and not give a fuck about any of them. To men, sex is all about getting our dick wet, and that's basically it. Now in my case with Taisha, I allowed her to get way too close, and the fact that she had my daughter didn't make it any less difficult. I broke the rules and I'm the first one to admit it, I fucked up. I let Taisha into my world and I can honestly say that after awhile I fell for her, hard.

When I first met her, all I wanted to do was have a little fun and fuck a couple of times. Even when she told me that she was pregnant, I still didn't give a shit about her; she was just a bitch that I was hitting on regular. I started to really take notice of Taisha once I saw that she was accepting the little bit of time that I gave her and my daughter with no complaints. I know it sounds crazy, but I fell for her because she really didn't pay me any mind, and she didn't question anything that I did. She never called me to ask me to come over. I just popped up and she accepted me. All she asked me to do was to take care of my daughter, and I did that with no problem.

Feeling like she was slipping away, I started coming around a lot more, and gave her a lot more of my time. It may sound weird to you, but I didn't want her sprung on another nigga. Call me selfish, but I don't give a fuck! Once I started giving her more than that, it all changed. She started calling me every day, asking me when I was coming by, asking me where I'd been, and I couldn't take that. Shit, I already had a wife; I didn't need two, and so that's when I started to distance myself from her and Moni again. The three to four visits per week turned into maybe two, if that. I wanted to distance myself, but I still gave her just enough to keep her around.

My ringing phone brings me back to why I'm sitting up on the couch at almost 6 o'clock in the morning. Seeing that it's Tony, I answer it with no hesitation.

"Hello," I answer.

"Are you watching the news?" he asks.

"Naw, why what's up?" I ask, wondering why he's calling me this early in the damn morning asking me about the news.

"Turn to channel 8," he says. I reach for the remote, aim it at the TV and hit the power button.

The lady TV reporter announces, "I'm at the crime scene of a murder investigation here on 130th in Tyler on Cleveland's west side." The reporter is standing in the street and continues, "Details of the crime have not yet been released, but police are saying that they have a suspect in mind. A warrant has been issued for the arrest of said suspect, who is the victim's ex-boyfriend and alleged father of her children. I don't have any more information at this time, so tune in at ten for more." The news broadcaster was finished, and my heart jumped out of my chest because I could see where she was. She was standing in front of Taisha's house. She couldn't be dead. She just couldn't be.

"Raimone," Tony says pointedly, "tell me you didn't have anything to do with this."

"I don't know what's going on," I stammer, not sure as to what's happening.

"Did you go see her yesterday after you got out?"

he asks.

"Naw. Yeah. Man, I don't fucking know," I say, frustrated.

"Raimone, I need you to meet me at the courthouse by noon, because they have a warrant for your arrest," Tony explains.

"I'm not about to go down there and turn myself in for some shit that I didn't do. What the fuck type of shit is this?" I yell into my phone.

"Listen to me carefully, Raimone," Tony warned. "I'm going do everything in my power to make sure you get out of jail, but you gotta listen to me. I need you to meet me by noon, so I can walk you into the jail to turn yourself in. They are going to arrest you, and we can sit down and you can tell me everything that you need to tell me. If you don't turn yourself in, you're going to appear guilty and you really don't want that. So please, just do as I ask," Tony pleads, and I agree to meet him there by twelve.

My mind is racing and instantly I think of Sasha. What if she sees the news and thinks that I had something to do with Taisha being dead? I mean, if I were Sasha, I would think so. I did tell Sasha that I was going to kill Naitaisha once I got out. Certainly if you looked at my face, it does look as if I got into a fight with a woman. Oh my God, I suddenly realized: My face! They are going to convict me without a doubt when I stroll in there with all these damn scratches on my face. If Taisha is dead, I'm pretty sure they are going to pull my DNA from under her fingertips, and that's gonna be the end of me. My head is spinning and I don't know what to do, so I call Sasha.

"Hello," she answers groggily, and I can tell that

she's resting.

"Baby, where are you?" I ask.

"I'm at Tasha's," she responds shortly.

"Well, I need you to come home real quick. I need to tell you something," I say.

"Is everything okay?" she asks, sounding worried.

"No, Baby, I'm about to go back to jail. I have to turn myself in by noon."

"Why!" she screeches and I can tell she no longer laying down.

"They found that girl murdered, and I'm the main suspect, but I swear to you I didn't kill that girl, Sash!" I cry desperately into the receiver.

"I'm on my way home, Raimone. I'll be there in fifteen, okay?" she promises.

"Okay," I mutter.

Like she said, Sasha is busting through the door of the house in fifteen minutes exactly. Her eyes are puffy and I can tell that she's been crying. It hurts me to the core to know that I'm causing her so much anguish.

"What happened, Raimone?" she asks. taking a seat next to me on the loveseat.

"I didn't kill that girl Sash, I swear I didn't," I tell her honestly. "I went over there to fuck her up, but I didn't kill her."

"Baby, tell me what happened," Sasha says to me, with concern in her eyes.

"Well I knocked on the door, and she opened it with this stank-ass attitude and I lost it. I slammed her against the wall and started kicking her and shit. Next thing you know, her house phone rings. I look toward the phone's direction and she bolts up the stairs," I explain and continue quickly. "I'm running behind her, but she makes it into the bathroom and locks the door. I'm trying to kick the door down, and she's on the other side telling me that she's sorry and that she didn't mean it. I ain't trying to hear that shit, so I continue to kick the muthafucka until it caves in. When I finally get the door open, she swings a knife at me, trying to stab me, but I block it and take it from her. I take the knife and place it against her throat and tell her that I should take her out of her misery right then." I act out how it was.

"I didn't come to kill her," I continue, "so I drop the knife and drag her into her room where I commence to choke the shit out of her. This is when she starts to scratch and claw me at my face, so I try to knock her ass out with a punch to the dome. I put my hands around her neck and eventually she ends up passing out. Her heart is still beating, so I know she isn't dead, but I sit on her bed to figure out what to do next. After a while she comes to, coughing and choking, but once she realizes that I'm still there she's starts to panic. Terrified, she starts to make promises telling me that she's going to go down to the station to drop the charges, and that she's going to leave us alone. I let her know that I never want to see her face again, and warn her that if I do, she's a dead woman, and she agrees. That was the last time I saw her, Sash, I swear. That girl was alive when I left," I tell her, placing my hands on my face to try to stop my tears. I didn't tell Sasha that I had also given Taisha twenty grand to relocate.

"It's going to be alright, Raimone," she comforts me, rubbing my back trying to calm me down, and I'm hoping with everything in me that she's right.

We end up resting in each other's arms until around nine, and even then I don't want to let her go. I have three hours before I have to turn myself in for a murder that I didn't commit, and it's weighing heavily on me. She is crying and so am I, but neither one of us lets the other into our thoughts. It isn't looking good for me and we both know it. I mean, I get arrested for the rape and kidnapping of this girl, and she's found murdered the day that I get out on bond. It didn't take a rocket scientist to figure out that I was fucked! I wipe the single tear that fell from Sasha's face, and she responds by kissing my hand. She then takes her hand, places it behind my head and brings me in for the softest kisses that I've ever had in my life. Breaking away from the kiss briefly and looking me directly in my eyes, she says, "Make love to me."

I pick her up and carry her into our room and lay her ever so gently on the bed. I then take off each piece of her clothing one at a time, starting with her shirt. After she was completely naked, she returns the favor and we both stare at each other's naked bodies without saying a word. I climb into bed with her and we kiss for what seems like hours. My tongue explores every part of her body and she moans softly, letting me know that what I'm doing to her feels good. When I enter her and begin to stroke, the sensation is something that I've never felt before, and I know she feels it too because she throws her head back with a moan as the tears roll out of her eyes and onto the bed.

"What's wrong, Baby?" I ask, as I temporarily stop moving to make sure that she's okay.

"I'm sorry, Mone, but it feels like we are making love for the last time," she says tearfully. I place my hands underneath her ass and dig deeper into her special spot, and kiss her deeply on the mouth with everything that I have. I don't know how much more I can take, it feels so damn good.

"Don't worry, I ain't going nowhere," I say to her, even though I don't believe it myself.

"I love you, Raimone," she says, as we climax in unison.

"I love you too, Sash," I tell her, kissing her softly on each of her eyelids. It's almost 11 and even though what I really want to do is lie in bed with her all day, I know that I can't. I have to be at the Justice Center in an hour, so I have to get myself ready to do that.

"I'm going with you," she tells me, grabbing my arm with her small hand as I attempt to slide out of bed.

"I wouldn't have it any other way," I tell her as I pull her up for one last kiss before I head to the shower.

After I'm done getting cleaned up, I walk into the bedroom to see Sasha drying off on the bed.

"I took a bath in the hall," she explains, reading my mind. Thirty minutes later we hop into my car, heading toward the Justice Center to a fate unknown. Sasha pulls up in front with about five minutes to spare. Seconds later we spot Tony pulling up in his money-green Navigator truck.

"Hello, Sasha, how are you?" he asks breezily, reaching out to shake her hand.

"I'm as fine as I'm going to be, considering the situation. How are you?" she says, returning the gesture.

"I'm doing alright, I guess. I understand that you're scared, but trust and believe I'm going to do everything in my power to make sure this goes as smoothly as possible. Are you walking in with us, or are you going to stay out here?"

"She's going to stay out here," I answer, before she gets a chance to.

"Why can't I go inside, Raimone?" she asks me with a confused look on her face. "What, you got something to hide?"

"This has nothing to do with something to hide, 'cause if you honestly think about it, the news is going put it out there anyway. I just don't know how this is going to play out and I don't want you or Raisha in the mix. If you walk in there, you're giving the reporters and everybody else free reign to get all in your face, and I don't want that. I've already brought enough bullshit in your life, I don't wanna future embarrass you," I explain.

"I understand, Raimone, I love you," she tells me as a single tear slides down her face.

"You know I love you. I'll call you when I get a chance," I say, kiss her one last time, and follow Tony inside to turn myself in.

Chapter Twenty-Four

Sasha

I fall apart in the car and bawl like a newborn baby as I watch Raimone and Tony head up the steps into the Justice Center. I can't think straight and I'm suffocating. This can't be happening. My husband can't go to jail for a crime that he didn't commit. Yeah, I said it. He said he didn't kill her and I believe him until he gives me a reason not to. Call me crazy if you want, but honestly I don't give a damn. Raimone is my husband and I love him with all of my heart. Yes, he's made mistakes in his life, but he doesn't deserve to spend the rest of his life behind bars. There has to be something that we can do, because at this moment it isn't looking good for him. I pull away from the curb, flipping open my phone to call Tasha. I know she's probably wondering why I wasn't at the house this morning when they woke up.

"Where the hell you been?" Tasha says.

"Girl, you ain't gonna believe me when I tell you: Raimone is back in jail," I blurt out.

"For what?" she wonders.

"I'm on my way there now, I'll let you know everything then," I say as I prepare to hang up.

"Oh," Tasha adds, "Mommy came and got Raisha, she said she missed her, so she's keeping her for a week."

"That's fine, I'm gonna call her right now and I'll see y'all when I get there. Keish is still there, right?" I ask.

"Hell, yeah, that drunk bitch is still here! Her ass is still in the room asleep," Tasha advises me.

"Oh, okay, well I'll see you in a minute, then." I say and press the end key. I then call my mother to see what her and Raisha are doing.

"Hello," my mother sang into the phone.

"Hey, Mom, what are you doing?" I question as I pull on to the freeway ramp.

"Playing with my grandbaby, and watching cartoons. What are you doing, honey?" she asks sweetly.

"On my way to Tasha's house. I didn't even know that you had Raisha until Tasha just told me. Don't tell me you over there lonely," I say with a smile.

"Lonely? I'm not lonely at all, Sasha; I just miss my Rai-Rai and I really wanted to spend time with her. I also know that you need some time to yourself," she says knowingly, and I instantly realize that she understands that things aren't right in my household.

"Well thank you, Mom, I really appreciate it," I say as I try to keep from crying.

"Good, Baby, you know she's always welcome here."

"I know," I start to say, then she cuts me off.

"Sasha, leave it up to God. He's not going to put more on you than you can handle. I keep my mouth shut, but I know what's going on, even though I don't always say so. You're a strong woman, I know you are. I just want you to know that your father and I are always here for you and your sister whenever you may need us. We're only a phone call away. We'll do anything in our power to give you all the help you need, all you gotta do is ask. I just want you to promise me that you'll call me when you need me," she says, sounding like she's tearing up.

"I promise," I say in a low voice.

"I love you, Sasha," she says.

"I love you too, Mommy," I say as I lose my phone.

A half hour later I'm sitting in Tasha's living room explaining to the both of them everything that had happened up until that point. Needless to say, they were both shocked at the news. A television broadcast interrupted our conversation and I motioned for Tasha to turn it up so that we could hear it clearly. An older gentleman was talking about a late-night murder on the west side and a picture of the woman I hated popped up on the screen. The scene switched to a young white news reporter and she was standing in front of an all-white house.

"Officials have finally released the name of the victim," she reports, "and she's twenty-two-year-old Naitaisha Bolen, who was sixteen weeks pregnant. Patricia Jackson, the best friend of the victim, found the woman's bruised and beaten body lying in blood on her bedroom floor." The reporter points at the upstairs window. "They are saying that the cause of death is due to multiple stab wounds to her chest and her throat being slashed. Police issued a warrant for Raimone Ford, the suspect in this case, who turned himself in today with his lawyer Anthony Peterson present. Mr. Ford is the ex-boyfriend and alleged father of Miss Bolen's two-year-daughter and the unborn child. So far we do not know what exactly Mr. Ford is being charged with, but we'll keep you posted. I'm Melissa Smith and this is Fox 8 News."

"Did you hear that shit?" Keisha says, the first to speak after the news story wrapped up.

I was in awe. I couldn't reply to what Keisha was saying because I was stuck on stupid.

"How the fuck can Raimone be the father of her two-year-old kid when y'all been together for nine years and his daughter just turned two?" Tasha wonders, staring at me.

"Your guess is as good as mine, Tasha; I don't fucking know. All I can say is that she told me this when I saw her. She just didn't tell me how old her child was," I say, and all I can think of is Raimone lying to me. Even though I was sitting in front of my family, who I knew loved me unconditionally, I was embarrassed. My happy little life (that everyone, including me, thought I had) was a bunch of bullshit.

I start to realize that I don't really know who Raimone is at all, because the Raimone I thought I knew wouldn't have done me this dirty. I tell them that I'd call them later, and I head home to be alone with my thoughts.

Chapter Twenty-Five

Raimone

A tall, middle-age black cop was screaming directly in my face: "How could you kill a pregnant woman and sleep at night? I know why, because you're a fucking animal!" We were in the interrogation room of the Justice Center. He was skinny with a huge nose, so he kind of reminded me of JJ from "Good Times" with those big-ass pink lips. The cop threw a couple of pictures on the table face up, for me and his partner to see. "Look at what you've done, you sick fuck!"

I'm sitting in a folding chair up against a metal table trying to swallow the vomit that's threatening to come up at any minute. I get sick to my stomach when I look at the pictures in front of me; pictures of Taisha's dead body. I turn my head so that I don't have to look at all of the stab wounds, or the look of agony on her pretty face. Who could've done this?

"Don't turn your fucking head! You look at what you've done!" JJ says, grabbing my face inside his hands in an attempt to keep my eyes on the pictures.

I grab his wrist and snatch my face from his hands forcefully. Standing up, I push him back with all of my might, causing him to stumble a bit before catching his balance. "Don't you put your fucking hands on me, man! I didn't do this shit." I can't believe this is happening; she didn't deserve no shit like this.

He walks back over, past his partner, and gets so close to my face that I can smell not just coffee on his breath, but also the stale smell of cigarettes.

"If you put your hands on me again," I promise, "you'll regret it. Just don't put your hands on me again and we won't have to see!" I look him directly in the eyes to let him know that I am not intimidated by his ugly ass.

He laughs loudly, "What the hell you gonna do, stab me like you did Miss Bolen, you punk bitch?"

"Look, man, I didn't do this shit, I swear! So you can cut all the sarcastic shit out, for real," I say.

"And what the fuck you gonna do if I don't?" he says, getting in my face once again.

"Look, man—" I protest.

"Officer Clark," he corrects me.

"Well Officer Clark, I don't know what the hell your problem with me is, but you've got the wrong person," I insist.

"My problem with you is, you're a cold-blooded killer who's sitting in my face, lying his ass off!" the cop says adamantly.

"You can think whatever you want, but I didn't kill Taisha," I say wearily.

He takes a seat across from me, crossing his arms in front of him, giving me a look that said he didn't believe me.

The cop's partner, a short Puerto Rican cat, finally speaks up. "Come on, Raimone. We know you did it. Just admit it and save yourself a lot of trouble." Like he really gives a fuck about how much trouble I am in. He's got a really slick and greasy-ass ponytail. Add in the thick goatee, I'm thinking his name should've been Rico Suave. I guess they were trying to play "good cop–bad cop," but that shit wasn't gone work on me.

"I ain't admitting to shit, 'cause I ain't done shit," I state clearly. "So y'all can get the fuck outta here." I waved my hand. I also flip the photos over, so I don't have to look at them any longer.

The door opens and in walks Tony, in a black Armani suit, looking dapper as ever. He closes the door behind him and takes a seat beside me. "Officers, do you have something on my client, or are we here because you can't find anyone else to harass?" he says, setting his briefcase on the side of the chair, sitting down, and folding his hands on top of the table.

"We have more than something, Mr. Peterson; we have this shit in the bag. Your client's fingerprints were on the murder weapon found at the scene, and we have a motive. Hell, he'd just gotten out on bail for her rape and kidnapping. We're also pretty sure that when they scrape up under the victims fingernails, his DNA is going to be there also. Have you looked at your clients face?" JJ said with a slight chuckle.

"What fucking murder weapon?" I ask.

"The knife you used to slice your ex-girlfriends throat! The knife that you forced into her chest about twenty times, that's what fucking knife!" JJ yells, spitting small droplets of saliva onto my face. It took everything in me not to put him on his ass, but I really don't need any more trouble.

"Like I said, I didn't kill her. You've got the wrong person," I say them through clenched teeth. This shit was getting on my nerves. They are sitting in this bitch wasting their time with me, when the real killer is out and about.

"Well Mr. Ford, tell me where you were last night?" Rico Suave asks, taking a seat in one of the chairs. I glance over to Tony, and he nods to let me know it is okay to tell them my story.

"Okay, I did go over to Taisha's house last night, but I didn't kill her. I kicked her ass a little bit, so that's why her body was bruised the way that it was. Shit, I was angry at her for filing those fake-ass charges against me, and I honestly wasn't thinking straight. So you're right, that's the reason my face is all scratched up; but I swear to you, I didn't kill her. I gave her money to leave the state and told her not come back. I also I promised to send her more money monthly to take care of her and my children. She took the money and promised me that she would do just that. She also told me that she was going to come down here to drop the charges, because she lied about the whole rape thing." The tears roll down my face as I continue, "I've been with Taisha for almost four years; I would never do anything like that to her. Yeah, I was pissed at what she did to me; but when I think about it, I honestly couldn't blame her. I've played with her feelings for years, not giving a fuck how she felt. So she did the only thing that she could do to try to hurt me: fuck with my family."

"So you didn't kill her, huh?" Rico says. "Well tell me this, Mr. Ford, how did your fingerprints get on the murder weapon?" He smiles slyly.

"I don't know anything about a knife. I never had a knife. Wait a minute. When I chased her up the stairs, she locked herself in the bathroom. After I busted through the door, she swung a knife at me, but I blocked it and grabbed her hand. I twisted her wrist and when she dropped it, I picked it up and placed it right up under her neck, letting her know that I could kill her if I really wanted to. If that is the murder weapon, that's the only reason my prints would be on it." I told them truthfully.

But by their faces, I could tell that they didn't believe a word that I had just said. "Come on, man," I argue, "why would I come in here and tell you guys that I beat the shit out of her, if I was guilty?" I ask, looking back and forth between the two officers.

"You'd be surprised how many guilty mu'fuckas tell us just enough to make it seem like they're giving us something. Then we turn around and find all the shit was a lie, every fucking thing. So what makes your sick ass any different?" JJ asks with a smirk on his face.

I was sticking to my story and they knew that they couldn't break me, so they book me and take me down to a cell.

Chapter Twenty-Six

Raimone

It's been eight months and I've been going back and forth to court for my trial. The good thing is that it's over and I'm waiting for the jury to reach a verdict so that I can finally learn my fate. I still don't know who murdered Taisha, so I'm really not sure where that leaves me. I know that I'm innocent and I hope the jury sees that, also. The prosecutor came with some shit during the trial that would make me look like the scum of the earth. I can honestly say that if I didn't know any better, I would think that I was guilty. The only thing that I got on my side is the lie detector test, which I passed with flying colors. They asked me all type of questions, which I answered with all honesty. When the question came up, did I stabbed or cut Taisha with that knife,

I answered "no" and it came back that I was telling the truth. I pray that's enough to get me up outta this mutha'fucka, cause I can't take too much more.

Tony did everything he could, but the Judge denied my bond, so I've been in jail since the day I turned myself in. I hope they hurry up, because this jail shit isn't for me, especially for some shit I didn't do. I think about Taisha all the time and wonder how Moni's doing now that her mother is gone. I lost my mom at an early age, and I wouldn't wish that on any child. It's just too much to bear. I was fortunate enough to have my grandmother take care of me, and she did a hell of a good job up until the day she died. I'm happy that Moni has her grandmother, Ms. Bolen, to take care of her; I know for sure that she's in good hands.

I had to finally come clean to Sasha about Moni being my daughter, because it was going to come out during the court proceedings anyway. I'd be lying if I said that I wasn't scared out my mind that Sasha was going to leave me. It broke my heart to hear her crying through the receiver when I broke the news. She cried until she had no more tears left and I felt like shit. She asked me a lot of questions that I really don't have answers to, like: Why was I with someone else? Was she not good enough for me? I explained that she was more than enough for me and that I was just being selfish when I was cheating. I promised her that I would never do anything like that again and I meant it. I'm not sure if she believes me or not, but I'll try showing her, even if it takes the rest of my life.

Even with all of the bullshit that I've put her through, my baby is still a trooper. She's always home when I call, and she's here for every visit. The news portrays me as a monster, but she doesn't let that stop us, she still holds me down. She's my down-ass chick. I've had to watch Raisha grow up by looking at pictures, and listening to stories about her. I won't allow Sasha to bring her up to see me. I don't want my child to see me behind a glass barrier, or have to talk to her daddy on a dirty jail receiver. She's getting so big and doing a lot of talking now, and I'm going through it because I'm missing out on all the good things. I'm hoping that the verdict is "not guilty" and that I'm out by next week so I can celebrate her third birthday at home with the rest of the family. I remember her second birthday like it was yesterday; what a difference a year makes. Last year at this time I was at home planning a big birthday bash for her and pulling out all the stops. This year is a totally different thing; I'm in jail for a crime that I didn't commit, and it's eating me up inside.

"Ford, you got a visit," the C.O. yells into my cell. I'm led to a room where I see Tony pacing back and forth.

"What's up, Tony, what's going on?" I question, as I see the look of distress on his face.

"The verdict is in, Raimone. I wanted to come down and tell you that myself," he says quickly.

"Ok, so what's wrong with that?" I ask, confused. A quick verdict is a good thing, right?

"When a verdict comes back quickly for a murder trial, it's never good," he says and looks away, pained. Instantly I'm dizzy.

"We have to be in court tomorrow morning at nine, for the reading of the verdict."

I head back to the cell in a trance. I don't know what tomorrow may bring and I'm scared. I'm facing life in prison if convicted, maybe even death. I honestly can't see myself in prison for the remainder of my life, I just can't. I head to the phones to tell Sasha before she sees it on the news.

"Hello," Sasha says after she accepts the call.

"Hey, Baby," I say sadly.

"What's wrong, Raimone?" she asks, concerned.

"The verdict is in, Sasha, and I'm scared," I admit honestly.

"I'm scared too, Baby, but we gotta believe that God is going to look out for you. I believe he is going to let you out of there, and allow you to come home. He knows that you got a family at home, and he's going to let you come back to us," Sasha says to comfort me.

"I hope so. I can't do life in jail," I say in fear.

"You won't have to, baby, just have faith," she promises.

I want so badly to believe everything will be okay, but that's easier said than done. I talk to Raisha and inform Sasha that I have to be at court early the next morning. She promises me that she'll be there, and we hang up.

Once I'm back in my cell, I stare at the ceiling. I can't sleep because tomorrow I learn my destiny. I get on my knees and do something that I haven't done since I was a child: I prayed.

"Dear God," I say penitently, "I know that I haven't talked to you since I was a little boy, but I need you now. I know that you see everything and you know that I didn't kill Naitaisha, Lord. I wouldn't do anything like that. I saw my mother murdered at the hands of the man she loved, and I would never repeat that act and forsake her like that. I'm asking you to please watch over me and make sure that the truth is found out and that I am set free. I have a loving wife and daughter waiting out there for me at home. I'm asking that you also watch over my other daughter, Lord, and make sure no harm comes to her. I know that I'm far from perfect, but I'm taking the steps to better myself, not only for me but also for my family. So I ask again, please watch over me and lead me in your path. In Jesus' name, Amen," I finish as I get up off my knees and climb back into bed. I'm hoping that my prayers are answered because I don't know what I'll do if they aren't.

Chapter Twenty-Seven

Sasha

I wake up around 6:30 a.m, a little earlier than usual. I have to make sure that I have enough time to drop Raisha off and make it to court to get a front-row seat. I'd like to sit right behind his table to show my support, and show that I have my husband's back. Today is the day that we find out if Raimone is guilty or not, and I hope that I hear something good. He's been behind bars for the past eight months and I'd be lying if I said it wasn't taking a toll on the both of us. Raisha hasn't seen him since the day he got arrested the first time. She asks about him daily. It kills me to have to deceive her and tell her lie after lie. I don't know what I'd tell her if they were to find him guilty today, and it's heavy on my mind. Breaking out of my thoughts, I start packing

Raisha's bag with everything that she may need for the day. I decide to let her sleep, because there's really no need to get her fully dressed this early in the morning if she's only going to go back to sleep at my parents' house.

Its 7 a.m. and I'm out of the shower, applying Vanilla Lace lotion evenly over my entire body. Securing the clasps of the black lace Victoria Secret bra behind my back, I then reach for the matching thong. Slowly I roll my nude stockings up each leg, careful not to snag them; I'm now ready to get dressed. I want to look sophisticated when I go to court with Raimone. My outfit of the day consists of a black pin-striped pencil skirt, white silk blouse, and matching jacket. I apply a light coat of makeup and remove my head scarf. Tasha did my hair last night in one of those long ponytails that comes to the middle of your back, and a short Chinese bang. The hairstyle made me look very conservative and that was the look I was yearning for. I wanted to keep the jewelry simple, so I put on plain, diamond-studded hoops, my small diamond-encrusted necklace, and my wedding ring. I grab Raisha's coat out of the closet, put it on her as she slept, and gently rested her on the couch. Sliding on my black pumps, I button my short black pea coat, grab my clutch, and I'm out the door by 7:45.

I pull up into my parent's driveway at around 8:15 and like always, my mom is preparing breakfast.

"Good morning," she sang, stirring what I assume is grits in a small pot.

"Good morning," I say. "Do you want me to lay her down upstairs?" I ask, lugging a sleeping Raisha into the house.

"No, baby, you can lay her in there on the couch,"

she said, pointing with her free hand. Walking into the living room, I see my dad sitting on the loveseat watching an old western movie.

"Hi Daddy," I greet him, shocked that he's home because he's usually always at work. My dad is a workaholic; he's been that way since Tasha and I was younger.

"Hello, Baby, how ya been?" he asks. I let him know that I'm fine as I place the bag on the floor and remove Raisha's coat. I then put her on the couch and place a small blanket that I found on the arm of the couch on top of her. I give her a kiss on the forehead; I then give my dad a kiss on the cheek and walk back into the kitchen.

"What's up with Daddy being home?" I ask my mom.

"He's thinking about retiring," she says, "and we wanted to see what it was like to be at home all day." She smiled.

"Daddy is silly, in there watching them old westerns," I say, laughing.

"As long as he doesn't ask me to watch them, we'll be just fine," she declares, placing a stack pancakes on a plate that I assume is my dad's. After pouring a tall glass of orange juice, she then adds bacon, cheese eggs, and grits to the already full plate.

"I know that's right, Mom. I never liked those movies either." I hesitate slightly and then say, "I gotta go Mom. I'll be back after the trial is over." I prepare to walk out of the door.

"Sasha?" she stops me.

"Yes, Mom," I answer.

"Whatever happens today is meant to be," Mom reminds me. "If God intends for Raimone to come home to you today, he will; but if God doesn't, he won't. Do you hear me?"

"Yes, Ma'am," I reply.

"If it goes the way that you want, you jump for joy. But, at the same time, if it doesn't, I want you to be strong. Don't you let them people see you break."

"I understand," was all that I could say. I plant a kiss on her cheek and walk out of the door.

It's 8:45 when I finally get through the metal detectors and am on my way toward the courtroom. I pull open the door, take my seat right behind Raimone's table and wait patiently for the court proceedings to start. People are starting to come inside sporadically and the courtroom is filling up rapidly. I notice an older woman sitting in the back with a small child and if I didn't know any better, I would believe that it was my Raisha. My breath gets caught inside my chest and I struggle to fight with the feelings that I have going on inside of me at this moment. My husband is on trial for the murder of his mistress and their child is sitting right behind me. I can't take it! I quickly lay down my coat to save my spot and rush off toward the bathroom.

"Excuse me," I say as I hastily brush past a woman and run into the handicap stall. I sit on the toilet, place my face inside of my hands and sob uncontrollably. What has become of my life? This is not the way this shit is supposed to go; I'm supposed to be happy right now, not crying on a dirty-ass toilet in the Justice Center. It takes me a couple of minutes to get myself together and to calm myself down enough to exit the stall. Walking up to the sink, I shake my head and pity myself at how bad I'm doing right now. Staring at my reflection, I slowly dab my eyes with a piece of tissue. Placing a couple curls behind my ear so that they don't get wet, I place both hands under the running water and lightly splash it on my face. Grabbing a couple of paper towels to dry the water, I touch up my makeup.

I'm feeling refreshed when I walk back inside the courtroom, with my head held high. I promise myself that I will not break down; I was going to do as my Mom said and be strong. Raimone turns to give me a quick smile, I return it and the bailiff speaks.

"All rise," the bailiff says and we all stand up. He then proceeds to introduce Judge Marshall, who looked to be around seventy years old. His skin is a pale color, and the robe that he has on is clinging to his frail body as he moves slowly to his seat.

"You may be seated," the judge says. He says a couple of words, and then asks the jury if they have reached the verdict. They reply yes, and the first juror stands up to read it. The courtroom is silent.

"On the count of battery, we find the defendant guilty," the juror reads.

Everything went in slow motion.

"On the count of premeditated murder, we find the defendant guilty," I heard.

"On the count of manslaughter, we find the defendant guilty!" he says aa he looks right at Raimone; I couldn't believe it!

"This is bullshit! I ain't killed that damn girl!" Raimone yells, trying to get at the jurors, only to be detained by three bailiffs. They drag him kicking and screaming through the door on the side of the courtroom. I look back in time to see the older lady smile at me and lead the little girl out of the door. I was stuck! They found him guilty of every charge, he was going to spend the rest of his life behind bars.

The room got loud. "Order in the court! Order in the court!" the judge yells feebly as he bangs his gavel against the stand. "Sentencing will be held on March 31. Court adjourned," he says as he gets up and walks away. Raimone had exactly four days to find out just how long he had to remain a prisoner.

For me, it seemed as if the next four days went by in a blur. I don't remember what I did or where I was. I was mindless, stuck in a horrible nightmare.

Before I knew it, March 31st had arrived. It's sentencing day and I'm back inside the courtroom awaiting my husband's fate.

"Do you have anything to say for yourself, Mr. Ford?" Judge Marshall asks Raimone before sentencing.

"Your honor, I have only a little to say" Raimone begins. "I'm innocent. I didn't kill Miss Bolen. It's really disturbing that I'm in jail for this crime that I didn't commit and the real murderer is still running free. I'm very remorseful for all of this, but I am not a murderer. Miss Bolen was not only the mother of my children, but also a dear friend. I would have never done anything like this to her, or to my unborn child."

My heart pounds in my chest. I couldn't believe he was saying these things with me inside the courtroom. Call it evil, if you may, but at this moment I hated her even more to know that she had a piece of my husband's heart.

Paying no mind to what Raimone had said, the judge had something to tell him: "Mr. Ford, I'm not even going to sit here and sugarcoat any of this, you disgust the hell out of me. Looking at the pictures of Miss's Bolen's body sends shivers up my spine. I found myself asking, how a man can do this to a woman and her unborn child?" The judge pauses for a moment and then says, "Then I'm brought to reality and I realize that you're not a man, you're a coward! You couldn't tell you wife that you've been cheating on her for years, and that this affair had resulted in a child. You couldn't tell her that this same woman was pregnant again with your second child!"

Judge Marshall sat up, and roared as his face was turning a bright red. "I don't think that you belong in society with normal people; because honestly, it takes a sick bastard to beat a pregnant woman the way you did, hell any woman, for that matter. What I think is disturbing is the fact that you can stand here in my courtroom and still tell me with a straight face that you didn't murder this girl. All of the evidence points directly to you; hell, your fingerprints are all over the murder weapon. They found your DNA under the victim's fingernails. The house wasn't broken into, so that leads me to believe that she knew her attacker. That attacker is standing in my courtroom today, and believe me when I tell you, Mr. Ford, you're not going to get away with this."

The judge is absolutely right and he didn't hold back; he sentences Raimone to life in prison without the possibility of parole.

Chapter Twenty-Eight

Raimone

It's been two days since I was sentenced. I still haven't accepted reality. This can't be my fate. I just can't understand what went wrong. Who killed Taisha? I don't know of anybody who would want her dead. This shit is unreal! I have a visit with Sasha today, so I'm going to straighten up and at least make myself look presentable.

"Sasha, poor Sasha!" I mutter to myself. I can't believe that I've put her through all of this bullshit, and she still makes time for me. I wish that I could really show her how sorry I am for all of this.

It's not fair for me to ask her to wait for me during a life sentence, especially the way that it came to play. This hurts my soul, but I know what I have to do and that is to let her go. It kills me to know that I will never be able teach my daughter how to ride a bike, or be able walk her down the aisle on her wedding day. How do you tell your daughter that you weren't around for most of her life because you made mistakes? How do you tell her that you got charged for killing your mistress and her unborn brother? I feel like shit because I know that I have failed my family. I didn't keep the promise that I made to my mother many years ago. I mean, I tried to keep Taisha and anybody else from hurting my family; but I am the person who causes them the most pain. Today I am going to put everything on the table; no more lies, no more secrets.

At our meeting, Sasha is looking like a million bucks today, and I let her know that as soon as I pick up the receiver.

"You look beautiful," I tell her with a smile, even though I'm dying inside.

"Thank you, Raimone," she says lovingly, with a grin. "How have you been?"

"I been doing as fine as I'm going to. Still a little shocked about the outcome," I admit.

"You and me both! I still can't believe it." She shakes her head from side to side.

"How's Raisha?" I ask, trying to change the subject because I am starting to get choked up. I can't break down in front of her; I have to keep my composure.

"She's doing good, walking around the house like she running shit," she informs me, giggling. I can't do anything but chuckle also, because I know my baby is a mess. Sasha continues, "Her lil ass gets any and everything she wants, I'm talking 'bout Tasha, Mom, Dad; shit, we all trip over our feet for her. Lil Momma is a D.I.V.A!"

"How's Mom, and Dad?" I inquire.

"They're fine," Sasha says. "Dad is finally thinking about retiring and Mom is trying to slowly take my baby from me. It's gotten so bad that she'll pick her up and tell Tasha that's she keeping her for a couple of days without even asking me."

"She does love her Raisha," I say, thinking about how gorgeous my daughter is.

"I know," Sasha replies, "that's why I don't even trip about it. Oh yeah, when I left this morning, Mom told me to tell you Hi."

"Oh yeah? Tell Ma Dukes I said what's up," I say. "So, how have you really been, Sash?"

"I've been holding up, taking it day by day, you know," she replies. "It's hard sometimes, but I make do, considering the circumstances."

"I know I told you on many occasions, but I am truly sorry for everything that I've put you through," I say.

She interrupts, "Raimone, I—"

"No, Sasha, let me finish," I state firmly, cutting her off. "I love you with all of my heart, and I can honestly say I fucked up! I had a wonderful woman at home, but I chose to go out and do other shit instead of staying true. I'm not saying any of this because I got caught up, but because it's the truth. I had no plans on being with Naitaisha, but I slipped up and she got pregnant with Moni and I kinda got stuck. I never meant to hurt you because you mean the world to me," I say honestly. "I know you think now that I was being fake when I was excited about Raisha, but I wasn't. Even though I already had a child, having one with you was always my dream. I knew that you were going to be my wife the very first day that I saw you walking down the street with Tasha's smart ass!"

She smiles through her tears. She pulls out a small Kleenex from her pocket and dabs at the corners of her eyes to catch the tears. I wasn't finished yet, so I continued cleansing my soul.

"I know you probably think I lied to you when I told you that the affair was done, after you left the house, but I didn't lie to you about that. I went to her house with a couple grand and I told her that I was taking care of my daughter and that we were done. She called me constantly, but I didn't answer because I was trying to do right by you and Raisha. The same night of Rob's party, she comes up to me and basically says what's up, and walks away. I'm shocked that she didn't act a fool, but I'm also happy that she didn't cause a scene. Anyways, after the party is over I come outside to find her with her head down on the hood of my car. She gives me this story about how her and her girls got into it, and she got left in the process, which I now know is a bunch of bullshit. I end up taking her home, but she's acting like she's sick, and by the time we pull up she's out cold." I say all this to Sasha, at the same time I'm studying the way that she's absorbing all of this information. She's void of any emotion and I'm kinda scared, yet I continue.

"I carry her in the house and upstairs into her bedroom to lay her down in the bed. She all of a sudden wakes up and asks for Tylenol and water, after I hand them to her, she asks me to sit down. I don't know what made me do it, but I did and she starts to kiss me. I didn't resist even though I knew that I should've. We ended up in the bed having sex, and when that was done, she sat up and told me that she was pregnant again. I lost it! I flipped on her and I told her that she had to get rid of it. I explained that I loved you," I continue, "and that I couldn't bring another child into this world unless it was by you. I threw some money on the table and walked outta the door. The next day the police come to the house to arrest me for her rape and kidnap. Now that I think about it, I really don't blame her for the extremes that she went through to hurt me, because I played with her feelings for years. I just didn't appreciate the fact that she brought the shit to you, and that you were innocent. Baby, I promise you, when Tony does this appeal I'm going to come home and be the best man that I can be. No more bullshit, just me, you, and Raisha."

"So you lied to me about everything?" Sasha finally asks in tears.

"Yes, I have lied about a lot of things," I admit to her, "but I never lied about how much I love you."

"You don't love me, Raimone. You love yourself," she says, pointing through the glass at me. "That's who you've been out for all of these years, your damn self! I was kinda feeling bad for the shit that I've done, but I don't anymore." I notice that she's not crying anymore. She looks like a different person to me at this moment, and it's scaring me, but I just listen.

"I told you not to play with me, but you thought shit was sweet and did anyways. Why did you have to fuck that bitch again? You wanna know, Raimone? Because you're weak. You let her pussy control your mind, and for that you have to pay the price. Unfortunately, that price is your freedom. You didn't do what you had to do to protect your family. But I did, because you're no longer in a position to hurt us anymore." She laughs like a maniac into the phone receiver, which sends chills up my spine.

"What do you mean, Sash? What the hell are you saying?" I ask, not really able to understand where she's going with all of this.

"I'm saying that there won't be an appeal. You're broke!" she laughs again.

This is not the Sasha that I know talking to me right now, she's demonic-like. I can barely believe what she starts to tell me, but I understand her saying at least this much: I've got all of your money; I've sold the house and your car. I'm taking my daughter far away from the shit that you've put us though. So you sit in here and think about everything, and tell me, was it worth it?

I see her stand up. She hangs up the phone and walks away. But she suddenly realizes that she forgot something. She walks back in front of the glass, picks up the receiver, and says something that makes my skin tingle.

"Oh yeah, that extra $20,000 I got from ya girl really made my stash grow. All I have to say to you now is: you knew betta!" She walks away for good this time.

All I can do is sit here, being stupid. I've been played. Sasha must have killed Taisha and made it look like I did it. And the ruse worked. You see, I never told Sasha that I gave Taisha any money, and even though I told the detectives, I never told them how much it was. Sasha got me with the ultimate payback; I didn't think she had it in her. I guess the lesson that I'm supposed to have learned is the hardest lesson known to man: Hell hath no fury like a woman scorned.

Yes, I was wrong for the way I played my hand with this whole situation. If I could turn back the hands of time, I would do things a lot differently. Of course I know that time travel isn't possible, so I guess I gotta live with the fact that my actions caused both women to lash out on me the best way that they knew how. I understand what it feels like to be made a fool of, and from where I'm standing right now, it doesn't feel good. My mind keeps going back to the things that they were both saying to me, but that I chose to ignore. Taisha had said, "If you continue to hurt me, there's no telling what I might do." And Sasha told me, "Don't fuck with me, Raimone, 'cause I promise you, you'll regret it."

Why didn't I listen?

Even with all that said, Sasha betta hope like hell that I don't make it out of this bitch alive. If I do, her ass is going to pay with her life, and I ain't talking about in no jail cell, either!

Chapter Twenty-Nine

Sasha

I know you're sitting there shocked beyond belief. But shit, I had to do what I had to do! I couldn't let him get away with the shit that he did to me, the way he embarrassed me, the way he made me look like a fucking fool. He thought that he could play these games forever. He thought I was just this naïve girl that he could tell anything to and I'd believe it. The funny thing is, I had his ass fooled!

I put my plan into motion when the police came to the house to arrest him. The name they said when they placed him in handcuffs made my heart drop. That was the same person that I had recently found out had ordered credit cards in my name. When the credit card theft department called me, I informed them that I didn't want to press charges; I had something better in mind for this bitch who thought she could hoodwink me.

Everything from the time Raimone got arrested was calculated by me. It was all a part of the game I played so well. The day that we coincidently ran into each other at my job couldn't have gone better; she thought she was so smart. I didn't know exactly where she lived, but I knew that Metro was her home hospital, so I did a little bit of research myself. When I found out she had a daughter whose name was Raimona LaShaunte Ford, it didn't take a rocket scientist to figure out that the little girl was Raimone's. Shit, their names were damn-near identical. My blood began to boil when I saw her birth date; it was almost a year before our child was born.

I sat in the bathroom of my job for almost an hour crying about the fact that I didn't know who I was married to at all. Here I was, loving this man with everything I had, and he was out making a second family right up under my nose. I couldn't shake the feeling that was taking over my body as I thought of the way he acted when we first found out that I was pregnant with Raisha. He pretended to be so happy about the fact that I was having his first child. When we found out that we were having a girl at my ultrasound, he talked about how nice it would be to have a daughter, and how he wanted her to be Daddy's little girl. I thought it was so cute how he named Raisha after him, only to find out that he already had a child whose name was very similar to his already. What kinda of sick bastard would do something like that to the person he claimed to love? Why would he want to make me look even more the fool, knowing I was naming my daughter almost identically to his secret child?

As I continued to dig, I also found out that his girlfriend was going to OBGYN due to her being pregnant again, which I figured was also Raimone's child. Because I had a friend who worked in that department, I took a trip up there on one of my lunch breaks to ask her for a favor. I knew she would do it, because she had just recently gotten a divorce from her husband who was cheating with her next-door neighbor. So to say that she hated home wreckers was an understatement to say the least.

"What's up, Sheila, how you been?" I said, as I stood on the side of her work counter.

She looked from the computer and smiled. "I've been doing ok. What's been up with you?"

"Trying to take it day by day," I told her. "Hey, Sheila, when is your break?"

"In five minutes. What's up?" she said.

"I need to talk to you about something very important, and I need a favor. Can you meet me in the cafeteria when you go on?" I asked, and she agreed.

Five minutes later she walked around the corner, sitting down beside me. "Ok, what you need?" she asked.

"Well, I just found out that Raimone is cheating on me," I said, stopping to let my words absorb.

"Get the fuck outta here!" she yelled.

"I'm serious. The sad part about it is that she's pregnant and she comes here for her prenatal care," I revealed.

"Pregnant? What the hell is wrong with him?" she asked.

"I don't know," I said, dropping my head to allow my fake tears to come.

"Don't cry, Sasha, it's his loss. You are too good for him anyways," she told me, rubbing my back.

"I know. I finally see that now," I said. "The problem is I can't get a divorce until I can prove that he's cheating on me, and the only way to do that is to know some information about her."

"What do you need? You know I got you," she replied.

"Just her address, so that I can follow his ass and take a few pictures," I said. "I also want to know when her appointments are, so, if by chance, he comes with her, I can catch him in the act."

"I don't think he's going to do no dumb shit like that—" she started to say.

"I just want to make sure that all the bases are covered," I said, cutting her off.

Thus from there I had everything I needed to know about Miss Naitaisha Bolen and I used it to my advantage.

The day of her appointment, she didn't even notice that I was standing not far behind her in the hallway while she was on the phone. She was telling her friends about her new baby boy, acting loud and ghetto, as if she were at home and not in a public place. She used profanity like it was the proper thing to say and even though she was dressed in the name brands, you could tell that she was the average hood rat who had struck a baller.

I couldn't believe Raimone wanted to fuck with something so trashy, but I guess that's what he likes. Why is it that dudes fuck with the hood-rat types? I mean, I'm not a guy; but if I were, I'd choose a woman who had a little bit a class. She wouldn't be a project bitch who doesn't want anything but to be somebody's baby momma, or a bitch that everybody you know has fucked. But that seems to be the type of woman these niggas want.

Anyways, I parked my ass directly in her line of vision, so when she turned around she would see me sitting there. I knew that without a doubt she would confront me, because that's what bitches like her do. I mean, why wouldn't she? Come on, now. This bitch was content with being the other woman for the past couple years, taking gladly whatever he would give her. So I knew the desperate bitch wouldn't pass up a chance to tell me every little secret she had, just to get me away from him. She kept her child a secret just to be able to still have him in her life; I mean, how pathetic is that?

Like I said, all of it was planned, and she fell right into the trap. She came over acting all ghetto, telling me shit that I already knew, but I played my role well. When I got fired that was the icing on the cake. I knew that Raimone wouldn't take too kindly to her having caused that. I knew that he would get out of jail, and go over there to kick her ass for playing her hand the way she did. So once I found out that he was out, I waited in the cut until he decided to show up at her house. It didn't take him too long after his release; men are so fucking predictable!

When he attacked her after she opened the door, I knew that my plan was gonna work. I waited outside for around thirty minutes or so. He came back out with blood all over his face and shirt. He opened up his trunk, grabbed a black bag and took it back into the house. A minute or two later he was back outside, hopping in the driver seat of his car. As soon as he pulled off, I jumped out of my car and walked down the street toward her house dressed in gloves and an all-black jogging suit. The door wasn't shut because Raimone had just walked out of it. I guess each had thought the other person had shut the door; either way it worked out perfectly for me.

Using my gloved hand to push the door open, I pulled my knife out and headed up the stairs. I followed the weeping noise to what I assumed was her bedroom, but I didn't see her. I could hear the noise coming from the bathroom, and as I was headed in that direction I noticed a knife with a little bit of blood on it. I'm not really sure whose blood it was, but I picked it up anyway. I folded my knife and put it into my bra. I'm hoping that there's something that links this knife to Raimone. Clenching the knife tightly, I slowly turned the corner and entered the bathroom. I stood behind her, unnoticed, watching her examine the bruises that Raimone had given her. It took her a minute, but when she noticed my reflection behind her, all the blood drained from her face, giving her a pale look.

"What the fu—" was all she got to say before I reached my arm around the front of her and dug the knife as far into her chest as I could; all that was left showing was the handle.

She tried to push me away, but she was way too weak from the ass-kicking that Raimone gave her. I pulled the knife out and repeated the process about a dozen times before she lost all of the fight that she had left and fell to the ground, face first. I took a step back and watched her there. She was not moving; I wondered if she were dead. A couple of seconds later my question was answered as she attempted to crawl to safety while still on her stomach. I took a seat on her bed, as I watched her struggle to get away. No sooner had I sat down on that bed, that I had visions of them fucking in that bed, causing me to lose it. I saw blood, her blood; I snapped!

I jumped up from the bed and ran up to her, kicking her in the side with all my might! "It's bitches like you who make it hard for women like me!" I said, kicking her with no remorse. She moaned and grabbed at the spot where my foot had just landed, as she rolled over onto her back. I picked my foot up and used the heel of my black Timberlands to stomp her in the ribs continuously until I'm sure that I hear them crack. I don't feel sorry for the bitch; in fact, I hated her. I hated her for sleeping with my husband. I hated her for bringing turmoil to my family, and most of all I hated her for making me do what I was doing at that moment. If she would've just left well enough alone, I wouldn't have been inside her home committing the ultimate sin: murder!

There's blood all over the floor, but I've never been one to have a weak stomach, so I was cool. By the looks of things, she was struggling to breathe. I watched her chest rise and fall at a slower pace than it did before. I felt sorry for the baby inside her, because I knew that he was just an innocent bystander in the sick game that his parents had played. I dismissed that thought quickly because I knew that this had to be done. I rolled her onto her stomach once again before standing over her. I placed one foot on either side of her body. I squatted and pulled her head back as far as it could go. Her eyes were closed, but I wanted her to see my face. Her last vision should be of the person responsible for her death. She should get a good look at the person she had thought it was so funny to make a fool of. I wanted her to see me, the woman she hated so much but wanted so desperately to be. My face should be the last thing that she saw before she went to hell.

"Look at me!" I yelled, causing her to open her eyes. Placing the knife under her neck I ran it across with all I had, and instantly I felt the blood oozing through my fingertips. I heard her gurgle as I let her head go and it dropped with a soft thud as the life slowly left her body.

Preparing to leave, I head to the door but notice on the bed the black bag that Raimone brought. I walked over to it and took a look inside; it's money, a lot of money. I wasn't sure how much it was at the moment, but I had plans on finding out when I got home. I grabbed the bag and took it with me, and the rest is history. The perfect plan right? Awwwww come on, you couldn't have pulled no shit like that off and you know it.

I may seem cold-hearted about the way that everything went down, but trust me, this shit affected me also. I loved Raimone, and I regret that it had to come to this. I'm also remorseful of the fact that I've killed another human being for something that she didn't do on her own. Even though she played a major part in what was going on, she couldn't have done any of the things she did to my family without Raimone giving her the power to do so. Since the murder, I've been going to counseling to try to get past this, because for a nice while I was having nightmares about what went down. I feel a lot better now that I've gotten everything off of my chest, because it was killing me, all bottled up inside! I wasn't a murderer and I don't look at myself as such; what I see is a person who was pushed to the edge.

I walked out of the Justice Center with a new attitude. All of this shit is behind me, and I'm ready to start fresh elsewhere.

I'm moving to Arizona into a beautiful four-bedroom, three-and-a-half-bath house that I absolutely love, thanks to Tasha's real estate talent. I got a house in Arizona for Tasha and Keisha: a three-bed, three-bath condo not too far from me. I bought my parents a five-bedroom, five-bath house in California, because they always wanted to move there. I made sure to buy them a big house because we need room to visit. Even after all of those things, I still have a couple of million dollars to play with, so Raisha and I are good. She turned three a couple of days ago, and we are going to celebrate at Disneyworld.

Naitaisha's mother, Ms. Bolen, died of a massive heart attack the day after the trial; I guess the older woman couldn't take all of the things that were happening. I felt bad for the little girl, so I applied for custody and it was granted. They said it was because I was Raimone's wife, and Raisha was the only blood family that Moni had left. Either way I didn't care, I just wasn't going to have the little girl growing up in the System for her parent's mistakes. Plus, I was the one who left the child parentless, so I took her in and treated her just like I treated Raisha: like royalty.

👑 👑 👑 👑 👑 👑 👑 👑 👑 👑 👑 👑 👑 👑 👑

It's moving day. I hop into the passenger side of the pearl-pink Escalade that I had just purchased after selling Raimone's car. Tasha's driving. Keish is in the back seat between Raisha and Moni. Those kids look so much alike, you would have thought that they were twins; all I can do is shake my head. With everything that has happened within the past year, I'm happy that I can give Moni the life that she so deserves without all of the bullshit!

"How'd it go?" Tasha asks.

"Just like I planned," I say as I lay my chair back, slide on my Dolce and Gabbana shades, and hit the road to Arizona.

THE END

P.S.

You can judge me all you want and say that I'm crazy and that you couldn't see yourself doing anything like this. That's easy to say when you haven't been put into the same type of situation that I was in. I was a woman who loved her family dearly and was willing to do anything to keep it together. That included eliminating the problem: Naitaisha. In my mind, with her out of the picture, all of my problems would be non-existent; but boy, was I wrong! The Naitaisha's of the world can only exist when the men in our lives allow them to. There are many Naitaisha's out there, they just go by different names and they come in all different shapes and sizes. What will you do when you finally meet her?

Acknowledgements

First and foremost I would like to give thanks to God, because without Him there would be no me. I'm blessed to be able to wake up each day, and I'm thankful for the talent that you've given me. I'm finally putting it to use.

My children Keiasya and Tre-Maine Miles: you both are the reason for every breath I take. I am so proud to have children like you! I wouldn't trade you for anything in this world. I got my dream on the first try – the perfect girl and boy. Mommy loves you!

My two additional children, Danea Campbell and Jenea Hooks: Even though I didn't give birth to either of you, I still consider you my children and I love you very much. Welcome to the family!

My mother Denise Johnson: Thank you for being a great Mom by raising all three of us on your own. You held it down. You went to bat for us if we were right or wrong and I love you for that. You are the reason that I am the strong woman that I am today and for that I thank you.

My step-dad Theodore Cunningham: thank you for stepping to the plate and being my dad when mine wasn't. Even thought I don't say it, I love you and so do your grandkids. Keep doing what you're doing, because you are greatly appreciated.

My brother Afonzo Johnson: you're more like a big brother than a little one any day. Always looking out for your big sis. Tell my nieces and nephew that Auntie loves them! I love you so much with yo' cool ass!

My baby brother Dennis: thanks for being my "on call" baby sitter. Even though you got grown on me and you don't want to do it as much, I still love you! You've helped me more than you'll ever know.

My beautiful little sister April Malone, I loved you more than you'll ever know. I'm still sorry that we couldn't see each other one last time before you left. If I knew what I know now, I would've made more time for our reunion. I know in my heart that I will see you again, just hold a seat for me. RIP baby, I love you!

Earl Hooks: thank you so very much for my beautiful children. I couldn't have done it without you, and for that I will be forever grateful. I also want to thank you for not appreciating the woman that I am, so in return I now know how a good woman is supposed to be treated. Thanks hon!

Jody Page-Wilcox (my godmother/aunt): Even though I don't see you a lot, just know that I love you with all of my heart. I still haven't met anyone as fly as you in my 28 years on this earth! I'm happy that my mother has a best friend like you in her life. Tell the rest of the fam I said "Heyyy," LOL.

Matie Weems: my ride or die bitch! We get to the point where we wanna kick others' asses, but somehow we end up back at it. Yeah we petty at times, but they know not to fuck wit' us! Tell my godson (DaChaun Anthony Pace) that I love him.

Cenora Thomas, my mutha'fuckin' nigga! Girl you remember our nicknames, Thelma and Louise. Twenty years and still at it! Can't nobody come between that, the saga continues!

Laura Hooks: even though you're not my blood sister, I look at you like you are. Years ago you welcomed me to the family and never let me go. I love you!

Antoinette Carter: you are more my Aunt than my blood ones! You are so quick to go to bat for me that it's ridiculous.

Remember this: "This mines right here," ... "Who the fuck are you?" (insider).

Victoria KoKruda: we had a late start, even though we were next door neighbors. You are what they call a true friend; you were always there when I needed you, and I know I've told you before, but I'll say it again, I really appreciate that. I love you, girl!

Nina Bentley: We clicked the first time we met with yo' "fly ass." Even though it wasn't that long ago, I know we'll be friends for years to come and even though I barely see yo' ass, you still my girl and I love you!

Dominique Russley: Even though we don't talk a lot, know that I love you very much. We gotta do a ladies trip...I'm thinking the Caribbean, what do you think?

Richard Lampley, you've known me the longest and I can honestly say that you love me just the way that I am. I ain't mad atcha baby, cause I love you too! Buddies since mud pies!

Jeremiah Jackson – you are the one who inspired me to finish writing this book in the first place. Hopefully you get yours up and running so I can read it. Thank you for your inspiration, much love.

Steve Andres, my newfound friend. I'm really thankful to have a friend like you In my life, you sure know how to make a girl feel special. Thank you!

Kawanna Mitchell: I can still remember the first time you made it known you weren't an ordinary neighbor. I was pregnant with Kei and you told that woman that if she didn't get away from my door with that B.S., she was in for a world of trouble. I know I'm known for my disappearing acts, but we always find a way to link up again. I love you girl, keep doing what you do (because I really need those pep talks).

Temperrence Grant: You keep me laughing till there are tears in my eyes with your silly ass! I haven't known you long, but in this little amount of time we've become close. Much love, boo!

My sisters Bernita and Ebony Johnson: I love you both even though I barely ever see you. Trust me when I tell you, I'm gonna get better with keeping in touch!

To Vickie Stringer: Thank you for believing in me and giving me a chance to do what it is that I do best. I will forever be grateful.

Acknowledgements

The whole Triple Crown Staff: thank you guys for doing everything that you can to make this book happen!

To all of the Jefferson Branch Library staff, especially Lil and Marcy, thanks for always keeping the new arrivals coming. You made sure I at least had a few books to read each week; you guys know how I am. Thank you!

Tammy Cannady, Carisma Warren, Shawn Warren, Eulanda Shayne, Kessiva Harries, Latoya Ford, Schmeca Ferguson, Stephanie Harris, Stephen D. Mullen Sr., Jessica Warren, Destinee Bentley, DeeDee Bentley, Antoinette Eichel, LaKoda Randleman, Jay Moody, Gladys Hawthorne and my West 7th family. Some of you are my Facebook friends, and some I know personally. Either way, thank you for all your words of inspiration. I really do appreciate your kind words, and whether you know it or not, you guys kept me pushing to finish this book. To all my other Facebook friends: I didn't forget you, there were just too many to name. Thank you.

To my friends at Kaplan Career Institute: Maya Smith, Crystal Middleton, Joyce, Christine Hernandez, Jackie, Nilsa Jimenez, Shawn, Lakea, Ms. Brooks, Mrs. Strozier, Mrs. Philpot and Mrs. Neitzel. Without you guys, becoming a medical assistant would've been a bore. Thanks for the laughs; I miss you guys so much! XOXOXO

To all you haters and fakers, you know exactly who you are. Thanks for doing what you do naturally. My world wouldn't be the same without all of you in my life. Thank you, thank you and thank you. Oh, and did I say 'thank you?' If not, thank you and God bless you!

If I've forgotten anyone, please don't take offense. It's because of my mind and not my heart (y'all know how forgetful I am). I got you in the next book. I love you all!

To everyone who bought this book, I also want to thank you. I hope you enjoy reading it just as much as I enjoyed writing it.

♖ Triple Crown Publications

Order Form

P.O. Box 247378   Columbus, OH 43224

Name	
Address	
City	
State	Zipcode

QTY	TITLES	PRICE
	A Down Chick	$15.00
	A Hood Legend	$15.00
	A Hustler's Son	$15.00
	A Hustler's Wife	$15.00
	A Project Chick	$15.00
	Always a Queen	$15.00
	Amongst Thieves	$15.00
	Baby Girl	$15.00
	Baby Girl Pt. 2	$15.00
	Betrayed	$15.00
	Black	$15.00
	Black and Ugly	$15.00
	Blinded	$15.00
	Cash Money	$15.00
	Chances	$15.00
	China Doll	$15.00

Shipping & Handling
1 - 3 Books $5.00
4 - 9 Books $9.00
$1.95 for each add'l book

Total $_____

Forms of accepted payment: Postage Stamps, Personal or Institutional Checks &
Money Orders. All mail in orders take 5-7 business days to be delivered.

♟ Triple Crown Publications

Order Form

P.O. Box 247378 Columbus, OH 43224

Name	
Address	
City	
State	Zipcode

QTY	TITLES	PRICE
	Chyna Black	$15.00
	Contagious	$15.00
	Crack Head	$15.00
	Crack Head II	$15.00
	Cream	$15.00
	Cut Throat	$15.00
	Dangerous	$15.00
	Dime Piece	$15.00
	Dirtier Than Ever	$20.00
	Dirty Red	$15.00
	Dirty South	$15.00
	Diva	$15.00
	Dollar Bill	$15.00
	Ecstasy	$15.00
	Flipside of the Game	$15.00
	For the Strength of You	$15.00

Shipping & Handling

1 - 3 Books $5.00
4 - 9 Books $9.00
$1.95 for each add'l book

Total $_____

♕ Triple Crown Publications

Order Form

P.O. Box 247378   Columbus, OH 43224

Name	
Address	
City	
State	Zipcode

QTY	TITLES	PRICE
	Game Over	$15.00
	Gangsta	$15.00
	Grimey	$15.00
	Hold U Down	$15.00
	Hood Richest	$15.00
	Hoodwinked	$15.00
	How to Succeed in the Publishing Game	$15.00
	Ice	$15.00
	Imagine This	$15.00
	In Cahootz	$15.00
	Innocent	$15.00
	Karma	$15.00
	Karma II	$15.00
	Keisha	$15.00
	Larceny	$15.00
	Let That Be the Reason	$15.00

Shipping & Handling
1 - 3 Books $5.00
4 - 9 Books $9.00
$1.95 for each add'l book

Total $_____

Forms of accepted payment: Postage Stamps, Personal or Institutional Checks &
Money Orders. All mail in orders take 5-7 business days to be delivered.

♔ Triple Crown Publications

Order Form
P.O. Box 247378   Columbus, OH 43224

Name	
Address	
City	
State	Zipcode

QTY	TITLES	PRICE
	Life	$15.00
	Love & Loyalty	$15.00
	Me & My Boyfriend	$15.00
	Menage's Way	$15.00
	Mina's Joint	$15.00
	Mistress of the Game	$15.00
	Queen	$15.00
	Rage Times Fury	$15.00
	Road Dawgz	$15.00
	Sheisty	$15.00
	Stacy	$15.00
	Stained Cotton	$15.00
	Still Dirty	$20.00
	Still Sheisty	$15.00
	Street Love	$15.00
	Sunshine & Rain	$15.00

Shipping & Handling
1 - 3 Books $5.00
4 - 9 Books $9.00
$1.95 for each add'l book

Total $_____

Forms of accepted payment: Postage Stamps, Personal or Institutional Checks &
Money Orders. All mail in orders take 5-7 business days to be delivered.

♕ Triple Crown Publications

Order Form

P.O. Box 247378   Columbus, OH 43224

Name	
Address	
City	
State	Zipcode

QTY	TITLES	PRICE
	The Cartel's Daughter	$15.00
	The Game	$15.00
	The Hood Rats	$15.00
	The Pink Palace	$15.00
	The Reason Why	$15.00
	The Set Up	$15.00
	Torn	$15.00
	Trickery	$15.00
	Vixen Icon	$15.00
	Whore	$15.00

Shipping & Handling
1 - 3 Books $5.00
4 - 9 Books $9.00
$1.95 for each add'l book

Total $_____

Forms of accepted payment: Postage Stamps, Personal or Institutional Checks &
Money Orders. All mail in orders take 5-7 business days to be delivered.